Acclaim for
The Gender of Inanimate Objects and Other Stories

"A dazzling collection—populated by strivers and grievers and criminals and romantics and cheaters and lonely-hearts—that is written in prose that is at once luminous and unflinching. Laura Marello has given us another book that is deeply thoughtful, totally human, wildly inventive, and downright haunting."
- *Adam Davies, author of* Goodbye Lemon

"In Laura Marello's *The Gender of Inanimate Objects and Other Stories*, people can be described by the brand of cigarettes they smoke. A Porsche can get poured full of cement. On any ordinary day, there can be a voice in your life for which you cannot find the embodiment. The welter of event and connection can make us consider bliss. There is bliss in recognition far more important than joy.

"Marello's eye is a crystal lens, not a ball or mirror. Her powers of observation are anthropological, and this anthropology includes the possible, the magical. Dialogue and events are created with exquisite reality and slant perspective. The readers immerse themselves in this invention—so great is her talent.

"Marello's use of the possible embodies the real zany possibilities contained in mundane, congested life. Marello's wit and eye are felt. We feel the old lady upstairs with fabulous but decayed history might debilitate anyone's ambition. We suspect the woman you have sought in your head, all your life, might reveal herself to you, but only as a voice in a video machine. In her explorations of the possible, Marello's fictions evoke Marquez, Calvino and Allende."

- *Paul Nelson, author of* Days Off

THE GENDER OF INANIMATE OBJECTS

AND OTHER STORIES

LAURA MARELLO

TAILWINDS PRESS

Tailwinds Press
P.O. Box 2283, Radio City Station
New York, NY 10101-2283
www.tailwindspress.com

Published in the United States of America
ISBN: 978-0-9904546-6-3
1st ed. August 2015

CONTENTS

for my sisters, Donna Graboff and Janis Barrow

THE GENDER OF INANIMATE OBJECTS

THE GENDER OF
INANIMATE OBJECTS

California, 1977

SPEAKING THE WRONG LANGUAGE

Think of Sweetwater County as a mismanaged four-square court, divided up:

Northwest

West

Southwest

East

instead of the usual. Imagine a large bite eaten out of the west quadrant, constituting Sweetwater Bay on the Pacific. Sweetwater itself is the beach town surrounding the bay; the Northwest quadrant contains the Sweetwater Mountains; the Southwest, the coastal farmlands of Guadalupe; and the East, the ranchland of Emeryville.

There is an array of maxims on the status of the Native Californian, the most familiar being, "There is no such thing as a Native Californian"; but I have heard a polar opposite motto, which appears to serve the same truth: "When you've lived in California for five minutes, you're a Californian." Take Sweetwater proper as an example. Since the primary industries in Sweetwater are fishing and tourism, the population (approximately forty thousand) consists of retirees, Sweetwater natives, Sweetwater lifers, Italian fishing families and wine growers, surfers, The Beautiful People (jazz musicians, hot-tubbers, young lawyers, realtors, and Szechwan cooks), the politically correct (Maoists, vegetarians, Moonies, herbalists, midwives, spiritualists, macrobiotists, nudists and reentry women), ethnic minorities, the sexually innovative (homosexual, humansexual, bisexual, transsexual, transvestite, asexual), transients and tourists.

The Northwest quadrant affords less variety. Sweetport, an old whaling port, is still fished by the Genovese. The Bank of Zurich owns the coastal farmland; they lease it to Tuscan sprout farmers and Chicano artichoke farmers. Inland, the Sweetwater Mountains contain ranchers, horsemen, wine growers, religious cultists, cranky artists, campgrounds and a nuclear missile base.

In the Southwest, the fields of Guadalupe nurture lettuce, artichokes, strawberries and Brussels sprouts. Chicano farmworkers nurture the fields. Emeryville is on the other side of the Coastal Range from Guadalupe, in the east quadrant. This is dryer land, inhabited by cowboy descendants of the dustbowl farmers from Oklahoma, who now own cattle and drive old Chevy pickups.

With this mix come various levels of cohabitation. You can ignore your neighbors. You can complain a lot. In Sweetwater, the Chicanos complain the Tuscans get too much attention. The vegetarians complain the carnivores' preferences dominate the restaurant menus. The artists complain the businessmen have destroyed their market-place. The Chinese farmers in Guadalupe complain their Chicano counterparts don't raise their artichokes properly.

You can acknowledge your neighbor but make him speak your language. You can learn Spanish and get a job with the County. You can enjoy the variety. You can smile and wave.

Before I drove a truck for Sweetwater Vending, I wondered how all these people got along. Now I realize they don't. Locals chase tourists off the beaches, throwing their litter after them. Environmentalists join hands at the entrance to the Nuclear Missile Base, blocking all traffic in or out. The Farmworkers stand up to the landowners, demanding fair wages and humane working conditions. Fishermen lobby to outlaw surfing in the harbor mouth. Gays protest that heterosexuals keep taking over their bars.

But they don't fight that often. Basically people keep to themselves. The retirees stay in their hotels. The surfers use the same stretch of beach every winter, read the Farmer's Almanac for tide reports, go to surfing movies at the public library, attend parties through word-of-mouth invitations. The Italians frequent Native Son dances, play in the soccer league, and attend monthly fish fries.

The gays dance at their own bar, the lesbians at theirs. The bisexuals hold monthly counseling meetings. The Maoists sit in their own café; the Moonies attend their own church. The mountain people rarely come down; the cowboys are hesitant to navigate their pickups over the coastal range. The Farmworkers are always working.

People keep to themselves. It seems the only ones traveling are the beer and bread truck drivers, the vending drivers and tourists.

Even before I got the job driving the truck, I was determined to learn Spanish. I thought it was all I needed to communicate with the residents of Sweetwater County. But Bubba at the job development program said to just cool my jets, because I had to remember that even though the deal was cooking, I didn't have the gig yet.

So I didn't learn Spanish, and the first four weeks in Guadalupe I wished I had. I see now that it would have been a first step forward, one of many steps. There is an equivalent population of Chinese and Italians. But even becoming quintilingual would not have erased the problem. It would not have helped me, for example, at

MacKenzie's Irish Pub in Emeryville, where the customers kept complaining, "Yantree grows mulreys, yantree grows mulreys," until they finally became discouraged and scrawled out *WANT THREE ROWS MARLBOROS* on a napkin so I'd fill the machine up right. It would not have aided me in Sweetport, when the barman at the Whaling Station informed me that we had reached a Mexican Standoff; nor at the jail, when a guard remarked, "Quit yer grinnin' and drop yer linen."

I have a friend from India who speaks a language that only sixty thousand Indians speak, a language that has no script. I, of course, don't understand a word of it. But when I get confused from too much truck driving I phone her and say, "Speak to me in your language." She does. It comforts me. In Sweetwater County, everyone speaks the wrong language.

CHAPTER ONE

Le Blanc on Infidelity

HTZ, owner of Sweetwater Music and Vending, started out as a financial consultant in Emeryville. He was commiserating with a client one day when the client, The Guardian Angel as my coworkers at Sweets called him, revealed that he had just sold some apartments and had two hundred grand to drop before the first of the year, to avoid paying capital gains. The Guardian Angel fronted HTZ the money to buy Sweetwater Vending.

Since HTZ didn't know how to run a vending company, and started by firing most of the lifers working there and infuriating the owner of Sweet Bowling Alley, the Guardian Angel decided to front HTZ the money to buy up the competition. At the start they bought Guadalupe Vending, Emeryville Music and Games, Mountain Music. They bought the Sweet Bowling Alley. A few months later they bought a motel in Emeryville and a condo in Hawaii. When a location wouldn't pay off a loan, or quit on HTZ and bought their own machine, HTZ bought the bar, or arcade, or whatever the location happened to be.

Then HTZ began revamping the inner workings of the company. He cut the personnel in half. He made Le Blanc route supervisor and gave him the music and games route (jukeboxes, pinball machines, video games, foosball, pool tables). Chester became the street mechanic, Hans the in-house mechanic and warehouseman. Tammy was given the entire full-line vending route (candy, coffee, soft drinks, food, frozen food), and I, Maya, was taken out of the office and put on the cigarette route, leaving Alice to do all the radio dispatching and secretarial work herself. I had only been working for Sweetwater Music a few months, and I'd never worked a vending route before. HTZ said Le Blanc had to train me himself.

On the first day of my training, Le Blanc smelled of Portuguese horse beans and apple pie tobacco. That distinguished him easily from anyone else. But if you rely on sight, be advised that he was short, used to be a wrestler, and had kept the bulk without retaining the prowess.

When we climbed into the cab of his music and games truck, with my cases of cigarettes thrown in the back, Le Blanc pulled down the blinder. It rained tobacco, beans, pipe cleaners, maps, paperclips, and his sunglasses, which were what he was after. As he pulled out of the driveway of Sweetwater Music and Vending and onto the highway paved through the Guadalupe artichoke fields, he caught me looking at him. He knew what I was thinking: at forty-two, Le Blanc looked sixty. He told me his father was a sheepherder in Bourgogne. He had inherited the old man's colitis.

What he didn't tell me, but Tammy already had, was that his first wife left him, taking their three sons, to marry his partner in their burglar alarm business. Le Blanc gave the business up and married Maria, a voluptuous Portuguese woman fourteen years younger than he, who took care of their new son Scott, and who he claimed had a bad temper. Once when Le Blanc got drunk, and everything fell down on him from above the blinder, he told Tammy that Maria had been married at nineteen, but during a fight with her husband she ran a red light. He followed on his motorcycle and was hit and killed in cross traffic. She saw it happen in the rear-view mirror.

We stopped at Luther's for breakfast, where we both ordered garlic steak and eggs, with a side of buckwheat pancakes. When the food came, he didn't tell me about Maria, but instead related this story on the subject of infidelity:

A man who drove a cement mixer had some free time and dropped by his house in the early afternoon, quite innocently, to say hello to his wife. Remarking, but not suspecting, the red Porsche parked curbside to be a visitor, he walked in the house to find his wife and an anonymous businessman, obvious owner of the red Porsche, in coital bliss on the now violated marriage bed. Without a hint of violence, the husband left the house, got into his cement truck, and before driving off, merely as an aside, backed the cement truck up to the Porsche and poured cement into every possible nook. The owner of the Porsche did not press charges. A few weeks later a more violent husband found the same businessman sleeping with a different wife. The businessman bled to death.

Further consequences were not discussed. Le Blanc only remarked that it takes two to tango, and that if he were in the same situation, as indeed he had been, he would be less harsh on the adulterer, and more severe, but never violent, with his wife.

After breakfast, our first stop was downtown, off the outdoor shopping mall, at the B&B Card Room. The B&B was a tiny gambling joint with close greyish air, a subterranean smell and an illicit feeling about it. Retired Sweetwater natives and their dogs occupied the card room. These gamblers huddled around the circumference of the slotted poker tables, clinking chips, shuffling cards, smoking and eating Milky Ways.

We unlocked the cigarette machine to the yelping of the dogs. Out of the twenty selection columns, ten housed Pall Mall Reds. Almost all the Pall Malls stored in the machine the previous week had been vended.

Our cigarette supplies consisted primarily of Marlboros and Camels; everyone I had ever seen had smoked those brands, so I was a little surprised. "Pall Malls?" I whispered to Le Blanc, in my youthful ignorance pronouncing them "paul-maul" instead of the savvy, streetwise and proper "pell-mell."

Le Blanc nodded yes, as if the predominance of Pall Malls at the B&B Card Room was as common and subsumed a fact of life as gravity or childbirth. "Card players," he muttered, splitting the cigarette cartons and stacking the fresh Pall Malls into the machine, "all card players smoke Pall Malls."

"ALL CARD PLAYERS SMOKE PALL MALLS?!" I exulted, like a toddler in a department store who embarrasses his mother by announcing with great relish that the man on the escalator in front of them is too fat.

Chips ceased to clink. Leashes grew slack. Chairs scraped and necks strained in my direction. I had revealed my naiveté to a group so entrenched in its habits that naiveté was not an option.

Le Blanc tried to show me how to split the Pall Mall cartons with one motion, stack the cigarette packs in two, and shelve them in two. Economy of motion saved a lot of time in this business. But I was too embarrassed now to concentrate, so I asked him if he could just fill this machine, and I'd try the splitting and stacking at the County Jail. He laughed and said sure, but it wouldn't be any easier there. When I looked at him quizzically, he shook his head and put his arm around me, as if to show me how much he really sympathized with my position, as if he remembered when he had to learn this job. Perhaps it had been rough for him, and he hadn't been half as green as I was now.

Le Blanc creaked the cigarette machine door shut, which set the dogs barking and broke the spell. The men went back to their games. On the way out, B&B himself asked Le Blanc who the pretty lady was, and if he wanted anything from the bank. Le Blanc introduced me as the new cigarette driver, said I'd be servicing the machines now. B&B chuckled. "And the bank?" he said, eyeing me.

Le Blanc said, Not today, and B&B laughed out loud, as if the joke was on us. I didn't understand a word of it.

Outside, Le Blanc explained to me that card players had been smoking Pall Malls since the Gold Rush. I scowled, seriously questioning the probability of this. I asked him about the bank. "Forget the bank," he said, and steered me by the arm into the passenger seat of his truck.

On our way over to the County Jail, Le Blanc told me that HTZ was convinced sales would increase if a "girl" filled the machines there instead of a man. There was no front entrance to the Jail. The front had been boarded up for nine years, and everyone—sheriffs, guards, inmates, probation officers, cafeteria workers, visitors and delivery workers—used the back entrance. We buzzed the back door and waited for Ralph-the-sheriff to say "County Jail." We identified ourselves. It was hard to hear because the Jail's back was turned to Sweetwater's most popular jazz club, on the outdoor shopping mall, and the bands often played outside on the latticed patio.

Ralph buzzed the door and it pushed open. We wheeled the dolly full of cigarettes and dollar bill changer equipment into a cage. They considered this the lobby. It boasted four square feet of floor space, walled in by the entry door, a gun vault, a barred door in front of me with a viewfinder beyond it, and an elevator to our right. We buzzed the elevator while the sheriffs inspected their new catch on one of the TV monitors.

"Who's the new girl?" they asked. "Why doesn't she unbutton her uniform lower? We got surprises up here on the second floor." Le Blanc just scowled into the view-finder and flipped them off. He told me not to pay any attention to them. He said they'd never pull that kind of stuff if I were alone.

Surfacing on the second floor, we emerged from the elevator, stepping into a bigger cage, walled in by the door to the kitchen, the elevator, a barred door blocking the stairwell and a barred door leading to a smaller frisking cage. Trapped in the frisking cage, I inspected our ultimate goal: the sheriffs' station, the hallway of glass holding tanks and the men's cellblock. The sheriffs taunted me less now that Le Blanc was visible, but there was something irresistible about an innocent trapped in their frisking cage. One sheriff told me to twirl around and raise my hands, so they could make sure I wasn't carrying any weapons. Another tried to handcuff me to the bars from the outside, but I managed to make myself small enough so they couldn't get to me. They handcuffed the dolly to the bars. When I complained, one of the sheriffs asked Ralph, "Do you hear a girl screaming? Isn't this the men's cellblock?"

Finally Le Blanc told them to cut the crap and let us out. When we were at the sheriffs' station he introduced me, told them I'd be the new cigarette vendor and they better clean up their goddamn acts. Ralph chuckled the way B&B had.

The men's cellblock had its own system of etiquette. When we arrived, Davey the guard took one look at me, said "Holy shit, brother, are you crazy?" to Le Blanc, and flipped the fisheye mirror out of range so the inmates couldn't see me. He whispered to me never to mention my name so I wouldn't have any trouble on the outside. Le Blanc told him not to scare me, and told me not to worry, it wasn't any big deal.

Le Blanc opened the cigarette machine and gave me a carton of Kools to practice splitting and stacking with. The cigarette machines in the jail vended mostly Kools, and then a few other brands. But when the prisoners heard the cigarette machine open they started yelling:

"Throw your smelly panties in Number Eight! No, in Number Nine! We've been stuck in the joint for months with no panties to smell! Didn't you bring us no smelly panties today? We don't mean washed panties; we mean used panties. We mean comed-in panties!"

A chorus of cheers rose from the cellblock. Davey told them to shut up, with expletives thrown in, and Le Blanc told me they were just doing it for shock value, and to go ahead and practice splitting the carton and stacking the cigarettes inside. I went ahead. Splitting the carton was pretty easy, except sometimes it ripped instead of coming open at the glued seam, and that caused trouble. Stacking the cigarettes inside was a little harder. You just had to twist them, about four at a time, from upright to sideways, so you could put about eight or so in the machine at a time, but I usually squeezed too hard, and the packs went flying everywhere.

The cellmates went right on though. "Did you do the laundry last night?" they said. "Strip and give us the panties you got on. Not comed in yet?" A second cheer went up. Bargaining started among the cells over who should do the work of getting my panties in the proper shape. "She don't wear no panties," someone decided. "Don't you wear no panties? Strip and show us if you got panties."

Ralph came in, and the Panty Litany halted for a moment. He asked me to turn my face to the wall while an inmate returning from kitchen duty stripped and was frisked for knives and forks.

"Face what? Put her face in what sheriff?" the cellmates went on. "Put her face in yours Sheriff?" The inmate was locked up, and Ralph left.

I went over to the cells to chat for a while. When I approached the men moved off the bars, zipped up their prison jumpsuits, and asked me was it sunny outside and who was playing that night at the Jazz Club. They asked me if I was going. I slipped them a few packs of Kools and some candy bars I had filched from the stockroom at Sweetwater Vending. As I left the cellblock they told

Davey he was in trouble now because the new cigarette lady just slipped them Mars Bars imbedded with razor blades, and he was gonna get sliced on their next trip to the showers.

As we passed through the glass hallway of holding tanks into the sheriffs' station we saw an old lady mumbling into her suitcase, an irate teenager talking to his social worker, and a young, angel-faced boy with blond hair and a dark tan, wearing loose white gauze trousers. He was kneeling in the tank praying. I asked Ralph what this underage vision of innocence could have been brought in for.

"That's Kenny Sears. He's twenty-one and strung out on drugs," the sheriff informed me. After filling the cigarette machines in another cellblock and listening to three verses of the Panty Litany I came back to the sheriff's station. The boy in the tank was waiting. He had stripped off all his clothes and was jumping up and down in the glass tank, thumping on his penis and waving it at me. I asked Ralph what he had done to that kid while I was gone.

"ME? You aroused him walking by his tank to the cellblock!"

"Aren't you going to put his clothes back on and take him to Detox?" I asked.

"No, we're going to leave him here, as a sort of celebration."

I knew who the kid was. I'd watched him surfing out at the Bluff. He was one of the best. And he was in high school. "The kid's sixteen," I wagered. "Why don't you give him to us and we'll take him over to Detox." But Ralph said, No way. I took one last look at the boy before we left. He had put his gauze trousers back on and he was sitting in the corner of the tank, waving goodbye.

One of the sheriffs had jammed the dollar bill changer, so we had to stay and fix it. Le Blanc claimed the guy had done it on purpose, but he said it would be good practice for me anyway. While he was showing me how to extract the shredded dollar from the mechanism's rollers, the guards brought out a chain as long as the sheriffs' station, and studded at intervals with handcuffs. I turned back to the bill changer and tried to forget it.

Some things are scarier if you don't look. As we repaired the machine I could feel the men being chained up one by one behind my back, the line getting longer, the hallway becoming more claustrophobic, that hushed static noise of shuffling feet increasing in density but not in volume. Fear paralyzes me, so I stood there with my back turned, fiddling with the machine even though Le Blanc said it was fixed, my ears tuned to the clanking of that long chain. I was waiting for them to shuffle out. Then a sheriff grabbed both my arms and got me into a half nelson. "Hey Ralph," he shouted, "We forgot one!" But Le Blanc told him to lay off, and he let me go.

The most frightening thing about the jail was that I realized I felt safe there, safer than on the outside. When I was in there, there was no outside. But the closer I got to leaving through the back door, the more appealing the outside became. Fright turned on me, and I was held in a terror of being trapped. The sheriffs, sensing every nuance of vulnerability, relishing the display of any foible, held us at the last door as long as they could.

First they told us through the intercom we had to wait because Ralph had to ask Le Blanc something. They asked me to wave goodbye, and tried to make me tell them I loved them. Le Blanc asked me who did I think was worse, the sheriffs or the prisoners. I said the sheriffs. Finally, I made so much noise beating on the metal gun vault and threatening to damage their viewfinder that Ralph came on and said, What about the bank? Le Blanc said, "Not today," and they buzzed us out the door. The first thing I noticed was how abruptly the air quality changed. The second thing I noticed was that the jazz music was still playing. I tried to ask Le Blanc again about this bank, but he just said I did so admirably in the Jail that I deserved a nice lunch, and he was going to buy me one.

While we ate our lunches Le Blanc just kept looking at me and shaking his head. I asked him what the problem was.

"No problem," he said. "In fact, you're quite a girl. I admire you." He watched me pour cream into my hot coffee. I told him I wished everyone would stop calling me a girl. After all, I was twenty-one and I had just graduated from college with a bachelor's degree. He laughed and said okay, but he kept looking at me that funny way, as if he were sizing me up, not in a leering way, but almost like a proud father.

"What's your problem?" I asked him again.

"Do you think the route's too dangerous, with the seedy card room and the jail and all," he asked. I said no. He nodded. "I thought it was at first," he admitted. "But now I think you'll be alright. You'll be safe," he said. I figured this would be a good time, when he was feeling sentimental, so I asked him yet again what the bank meant.

"You'll only be safe if you don't know, so quit asking," he said. Then he patted me on the head. "Time to go." When I complained again that he was treating me like a kid, he swore and said he didn't know how to treat me. Then he grabbed me by the arm and kissed me on the forehead. "Is that better?"

I just shrugged. "What are you so upset about?" I said.

"I don't know," he said. "I'm not upset about anything. I just didn't expect you to be such a great kid."

Le Blanc smiled like he knew something I didn't. But that was okay. A lot of guys wouldn't have even given me a chance on that route. They would have made me feel stupid and inept, in addition to being naive. Le Blanc wasn't like that.

Drinking and Going Blind

By the time we were halfway to the shop, I was pretty adept at splitting cartons and stacking the cigarettes inside. I practiced in the truck on the way home, and only sent the packs flying once or twice. Le Blanc said not to worry, no one got the hang of it the first day. When I kept practicing he told me I was overzealous, that it would just take a while, and asked me what I was trying to prove. I told him nothing. Nothing. And then I tried stacking the cigarettes again.

But splitting cartons and stacking cigarette packs wasn't the only thing I had to learn. There was also a fine science to getting the cigarette machine doors open. You'd think you could just turn the lock and the door would pop free, but no. Most of the machines had been banged up from bar brawls or from being moved from one location to the other. Many of the locks were sticky from beers and Cokes being spilled on them, or from smoke resin, or who knows what. So they all stuck or jammed when you tried to unlock them, and they all needed some special trick to be opened. Some only required a simple knee kick right under the lock, to free up the inside latch. That was the easiest. I only had to perfect my aim and thrust—just under the lock, not too hard, not too gentle. But other locks had to be rattled a particular way when you knee-kicked them, and still others had to be rattled and lifted when you kicked them. So it was becoming complicated. As we rode home I tried to memorize the particular combination of kicks, rattles and lifts I needed at each location.

"Knee pads," I said. Le Blanc looked up. We were passing the Pacific Gas and Electric plant at Guadalupe Landing. It reminded me of the new art museum in Paris, the one named after Georges Pompidou.

"Knee pads?" Le Blanc said.

I nodded, and he pulled down the blinder for his pipe tobacco. I told him I would need them to get those machines open. He thought he might have a pair in the shop.

I was still practicing my cigarette pack stacking techniques, and had almost perfected my study of the correlation between socioeconomic factors and cigarette brand. In just one day the diverse cultures of Sweetwater County had become clear to me, boiled down to their cigarette brands. The card players at the B&B Card Room smoked Pall Malls. The blacks at the Jail smoked Kools. The Chicanos at the Mushroom Farm smoked Winstons. The lawyers and environmentalists who attended conventions at the Oceansport Inn smoked Benson Hedges, and any other long or light cigarettes. The mountain men at the Whaler Bar smoked Camels unfiltered. Everyone else smoked Marlboro-box. Life was so simple. But I decided to wait awhile, to expand and confirm my study, before I presented the data to Le Blanc.

"Are you fretting about this stuff?" he asked me as we turned into the parking lot at Sweetwater Music.

"No," I said.

"Then what are you scowling about?"

"I was thinking about the correlation of cigarette preferences and certain socioeconomic factors in the County," I explained to him.

"Jesus Christ," he said.

"Excuse me?" I said.

"Where did you go to college?" he said. We got out of the truck. "And what was your major?"

"Vassar. Cultural Anthropology."

"How did you end up here?" he said. He opened the safe in the truck, and started pulling out the bags of coins we'd collected from the cigarette machines.

"I grew up here," I said. "I came back."

Inside the shop, Le Blanc showed me how to run the coins through the counter and fill out the receipt tags for each location. Then we drew up a stock order for the cigarettes I would need the next day, and went into the warehouse where the route drivers collected in the afternoons to sit and gripe while they watched Hans, the warehouseman, fill their orders.

Hans was probably the most endearing man at our shop because, when I asked him to put his shirt on, he blushed, instead of engaging me in a preliminary invitational headlock as Chester the street mechanic would do.

He said he kept his violence under wraps now that he had a wife and a baby daughter. He said he did it by reading science fiction and telling stories. When I had worked in the office I came in on my lunch break to hear them. His favorite stories were: how he saved the Provost Marshal from being killed in Vietnam by swerving the jeep and ducking to avoid bullets, how his swim teammates used to drown football players by tying them to the drain at the bottom of the pool, how he and other Sweetwater beach lifeguards used to rub Ben-Gay inside each other's swimsuit crotches to burn each other's nuts, and how he used to stock a Quaalude warehouse in Sweetport, where he sold to the Hell's Angels. He said it was all behind him now, dropping out of school, the Hell's Angels, heroin addiction, Vietnam. He called it a chain reaction: the Angels curing him of school, addiction of the Angels, Vietnam of the addiction, his baby daughter of Vietnam. He wore an anchor around his neck, the symbol of the Nordic God, Thor. He said it meant he was staying put now, a Guadalupe native.

So Le Blanc and I sat down on some cases of Snickers bars with Tammy and Alice, and watched Hans load the next day's supplies on a dolly for each driver. News and rumors were exchanged. Tammy, the only full-line vending driver left after the company upheaval, was warning Alice that the company was going into the hole eight thousand dollars a month on unpaid bills. That was the current and most habitual rumor. Alice, who responded to most everything with incredulity, asked Le Blanc what he thought.

Le Blanc shrugged. "If the refinancing doesn't come through, and the books aren't balanced soon, the mafia guys will start dropping by to peruse the books and scrutinize the route drivers' coin counting techniques." Hans nodded his head and tugged at the anchor around his neck. Tammy lit a cigarette, taking a long draw on it and watching the tobacco and paper pop and burst as it caught fire. I wondered if there was really mafia in Sweetwater County, or if Le Blanc was just having some fun with Alice.

"Nobody's touching my ledger," Alice squawked. "She ain't opening her pretty little covers for any of them."

Le Blanc and Tammy smiled at her as if they knew better. Hans shook his head. Alice looked to me for support but I just threw up my hands. What did I know? "Well, what about the comptroller?" Alice said. "Isn't he going to do something?"

"He's drinking more and more," Le Blanc said.

"He can't see," Tammy said. She got up, took her dolly and order sheet from Hans, and began to check the supplies against the list.

"He's going blind," Hans explained, and started stacking my cigarettes on a dolly. I looked at the brands and wondered where Le Blanc would be taking me the following day, which bars and clubs and bowling alleys and diners. Maybe the next day's route would enlighten my study on the socioeconomic breakdown of cigarette smokers in Sweetwater County. The prospect cheered me.

"He's still juggling the books," Le Blanc said. But HTZ was calling Alice back to the office—Chester was on the radio about some problem with the coffee machine at the Guadalupe Post Office, and had to talk to her that minute.

After Alice had left, Tammy squinted when she took a drag on her cigarette, as if she were scrutinizing me, and asked Le Blanc how my first day went. It struck me then that we were the only route drivers left, Tammy on full-line, me, a novice, on cigarettes, and Le Blanc on music and games. "She did alright for her first day," Le Blanc said. He looked over at me. I kicked the case of Snickers under my feet. "She's okay."

"They're not eating her alive?" Tammy asked him. She inspected me anew, as if she didn't quite trust me.

"Oh, they're trying," Le Blanc laughed. "You should have seen it at the Jail. Holy mother of shit," he said. Then laughed harder.

I was embarrassed, but then Tammy said straight to me, "Don't let them get to you honey, you stick up for yourself."

Le Blanc stopped laughing and asked her how it went, being all alone with the full-line route. "Well," she said, "I didn't have time to buy milk, eggs, ice cream and

24

sandwiches for those damn machines at the frozen food plant, so I'm going to have to do that on my way home. I tried to get Alice to help, but she has to get office supplies and go to the bank after work, since Maya isn't in the office with her anymore."

"I don't have an answer," Le Blanc said, shaking his head. "I'm not finished with my route, what with showing Maya hers, and I've got service calls tonight."

Hans laughed. "I bet Chester will leave you some mess," he said. It was Chester's first day as the street mechanic. He used to work in the shop repairing machines, and Hans was always being called out of the warehouse to help him.

Tammy wheeled her dolly out to her truck. "Now don't let them eat you alive," she called back to me. She threw her cigarette butt down on the asphalt, and ground it in with her boot for emphasis. I nodded.

Hans had finished getting our order up, and Le Blanc showed me how to check my list against the cases of cigarettes. Then we wheeled it out on the driveway and he showed me how to split open the cases so they'd be halved and the cartons exposed when I stacked them in my truck. While I was slicing cartons, Alice came rushing out of the office and gathered us all into a huddle behind Tammy's truck. She told us that she would be damned if the comptroller hadn't opened the curtains to his office, and revealed some Tax Man, from the Internal Revenue

Service, who had been there since 10am and was still poring over the books.

We stayed behind the truck and lapsed into frenzied speculation as to how deftly our comptroller had balanced the books and whom HTZ would come down on if the Tax Man found flaws. According to Alice he hadn't found anything yet, but HTZ was prowling through the old broken-down machines in the back room to distract himself, pulling tubes out of the coffee machines and stacking up broken PC boards on an old pinball machine.

I stopped speculating a moment to examine an Army helicopter performing its routine buzzing. Our shop was located near the Coast Highway in Guadalupe, and the Army planes and helicopters from the base in Emeryville constantly buzzed the area. It seemed there had been an unusually high number of planes and copters in the area that afternoon, but I discounted the notion, convinced that my imagination was fueled by the group's skittish paranoia over the Tax Man. I was accustomed to seeing small civilian helicopters with one major rotor over the bubble cockpit, but these Army copters seemed enormous; even with twin rotors I couldn't imagine how they carried the bulk and kept themselves aloft. Watching that day, it seemed like an awkward and precarious defiance of gravity.

Helicopters had never frightened me. The only things I associated them with were wind and astronaut splash-downs. I was about to ask Le Blanc what the aerodynamics were on these strange contraptions, when I was struck dumb by the fact that the group's skittishness had now been redirected: still acting as a unit, all eyes had turned toward the copter.

Just as soon as it had captured everyone's attention, the helicopter popped its front rotor and began to nosedive.

It is amazing how much time you have to think in the thirty-second interval between the moment a helicopter pops its rotor and the moment it crashes. First I ran into the street, but Hans yelled, "Take cover!" so I ran under the garage door of the shop. As soon as I arrived Le Blanc came screaming through the office yelling, "Outside, outside, the gas mains!" and remembering that we did indeed have two full pumps in our parking lot, I ran outside again. Hans had time to argue that gas mains or not it would be safer inside, because of the falling debris. I just threw up my hands and stayed put, unable to decide what difference it made if I were crushed by a collapsing warehouse or blown up by an exploding pipeline. As I watched the helicopter spiral down, I thought about the near disasters in my life: the time the earthquake threw me out of bed, the time I listened to the newscaster announce my housing tract had been burned down, the time my car blew up on the Ventura Freeway, the time I got lost in the Sweetwater Mountains for three hours after sunset.

The loose rotor lodged itself in some telephone wires above one of the four gas stations that framed the clover-leaf freeway on-ramp intersection. All of Guadalupe seemed to emerge from its respective indoors at the moment of the explosion and run toward the flames as if it were fleeing safety. I stood in the road with Le Blanc and held onto his elbow as we watched the Guadalupe children go by, pulling each other in wagons, pushing themselves on tricycles, bringing along their dolls and inner-tubes and half-empty Coke bottles. No one tried to keep them away.

The Tax Man went screeching out there too, his legs stiff and his arms held out straight as if he were trying to catch the flying shrapnel, as if he'd been shot in the back. When he returned we all followed him into the office. He reported that all three pilots were killed, the copter exploded on the freeway on-ramp, no one else was injured, and there were pieces of arms and legs everywhere. Then he burst into tears, gathered his papers and briefcase and fled, mumbling apologies and something about having been on the front lines in Vietnam.

I immediately looked around for Hans. Tammy noticed me and said he had excused himself right after the explosion and had gone home sullen, gnawing on his anchor. I sat down in the office and started to cry. Tammy offered me a cigarette. Alice offered me a doughnut. Tammy wondered out loud why the army didn't restrict its test runs to non-residential areas. Le Blanc said it was a damn shame, but the rotors popped all the time like that. HTZ was shut up with the comptroller in his office, whispering over the ledgers the Tax Man had abandoned. We quieted down to see if we could hear what they were saying. The comptroller was trying to assure HTZ that we weren't in any danger, that the helicopter had crashed soon enough, when HTZ noticed we were all staring at him. He stormed over to the door and threw it open. "Where the hell has the Tax Man gone off to?" he shouted. We shrugged. Alice tried to explain that the helicopter crash had upset him but HTZ cut her off. "Whoever was the last mechanic to check out that copter is gonna get his ass reamed," HTZ yelled. He shut the door, and the curtains. After that we could still hear them whispering, but we couldn't make out what they were saying.

Le Blanc shrugged. "The Tax Man, the mafia, we'll be down the tubes one way or another," he said.

"Oh stop it," Alice said, "the child's upset already, and you're just making it worse." She pointed to me.

"You want to go over to the Guadalupe Hotel and have a drink?" Le Blanc asked.

"You can't have a drink," Alice said. "It's five o'clock. You've gotta take over the service calls. Chester's off."

"Well get him on the horn and see what he's left me," Le Blanc said. "Sorry kid," he said to me.

"Maybe you should take her with you," Tammy said. She took a long draw on her cigarette. I couldn't believe how much she smoked. I looked at the brand. Chesterfields. Nobody smoked Chesterfields. She was in some socioeconomic category that I didn't even know existed. And all of the people in her category smoked Chesterfields. It was a revelation.

"You want to go?" Le Blanc said.

"Sure," I said.

"Really?" he said.

"I need distraction," I said.

"She wants to go," Tammy said. "So let her go."

Alice finally got Chester to answer her radio calls. He said he had just dropped his master keys down the elevator shaft at the County Psychiatric Unit, and all the patients were crowding the halls, trying to watch the maintenance men fish the keys out. Le Blanc went over to the radio and turned the sound down. "If HTZ hears, the Professor will get fired," he said.

Chester was once a policeman in Guadalupe, but he got fired. He tried to contest the firing but lost in court. Then he went to work for an electronics firm but was also fired. After that he went north to earn his Master's degree in Clinical Psychology, but dropped out of the program a semester before he would have graduated. That's why Le Blanc called him the Professor. Now he was working at Sweetwater Music, learning to be a mechanic, rewiring pinball machines and unjamming cigarette packs. HTZ had just put him out on the street by himself. It was a lonely apprenticeship.

Le Blanc got on the radio, told Chester to leave the master keys and come back to the shop. Le Blanc would pick the keys up after dinner. Then he asked for the list of calls Chester hadn't had a chance to complete.

I was glad we would be gone by the time Chester arrived. When Chester dropped into the shop in the late afternoon, he invariably got me into a Guadalupe Police Force combination arm and head lock, then asked me why my back muscles were so developed, what size bra I wore, and what difference there was between the letter size and the number size. When he released me he asked which beach I sunbathed at, and why I didn't use the nudist beaches past Sweetport. He concluded by telling me that he was a nudist, and his "lady friend" a sex therapist. Since most Sweetwater residents mention in passing that they go to Sweetport Dunes to enjoy the new legality of no bathing suits, I wondered why Chester exclaimed with a cultist's zeal that he belonged to a group of nudists. If he weren't such a bumbler, I would have expected him to become a guru and attract a large following.

Since Chester was backed up on service calls, Le Blanc and I had our evening planned for us. We needed to sell hand talc and cue chalk to the Blue Lagoon disco, unclog the sugar in the coffee machine at the Guadalupe Post

Office. The *Atlantis* pinball at Harvey's was registering free games, someone had taken the gear-shift knob off the *Indy 500* at the Sweetwater Bowling Alley, and a little boy had dropped his mother's keys down the exposed shaft of the gear-shift. Snowy Laundry wanted their jukebox disconnected so they could re-carpet at five the next morning. Le Blanc had it all written down.

"Jesus Christ," Alice said when Le Blanc got off the radio.

"An average day," Le Blanc said. "You ready, Kid?"

I nodded. "Have a good time you two," Tammy said.

The Duke is Dead

The Guadalupe Post Office was already closed, so we fixed the *Atlantis* pinball at Harvey's, picked up Chester's keys at the Psychiatric Unit and then headed over to the Blue Lagoon disco.

The Blue Lagoon had to be appreciated in its context—its competition. Sailor's Port was predictably meat market, i.e., men choosing women, and not just to dance with mind you. The New You Lounge was jazzy and self-conscious. There were few alternatives for ambience in Sweetwater. Plus, while the Sailor's was relentlessly meat market and the New You relentlessly jazzy, the Blue Lagoon was subject to endless revamping, redecorating, and upheavals in clientele. It sighed, burst, inhaled, and heaved.

In the early seventies, when I was home from college on summer break and got in with the help of my sister's fake I.D., the Blue Lagoon was a haven for Sweetwater's burgeoning theatre crowd. This group was comprised of large jolly women with ornamental jewelry and garish scarves, skinny pale men in leotards, glitter eye shadow and arched backs. These worshippers of illusion donned repetitive names like Jeannette Jeannette or muddled foreign titles like Ashley Ciarello.

Next phase: the pre-disco gays. This included a lot of short haircuts, mustaches, sleeveless undershirts, medallions, tight jeans and bar action. Johnny, our resident barman and coastal cowboy, was slick and attuned to the coming disco. He would lead the shyer boys through the new steps. For serious dancing, he paired with a short blond girl who had a pixie face and an adorable sway back, and was the only regular who knew the steps as well as he. The other barman at that time was blond and frenetic, and never abandoned his falsetto.

This phase ended when "breeders" or heterosexuals overran the Blue Lagoon. The present regulars still talked about this as an event, as older people might talk of the Depression or of World War II. There was nowhere left for the regulars. Long lines of disco dancers crowded the floor, moving in block formation, performing the same six military steps hour after hour.

But nothing lasts forever. An old regular of the Lagoon's gay days bought the Lagoon and invested enough money in the new post-disco gay-sleaze that he discouraged heterosexuals from coming back in unmanageable droves. The colorful jungle murals were blacked out and replaced by a mosaic blue-glitter lagoon. Funeral lilies and other swamp lore were dredged up. Clouds and cobwebs draped the ceiling. A slide show was introduced. The Blue Lagoon was re-launched.

Brent, the new owner, even changed his image. As a regular, he came shirtless, in a Levi jacket and Levis, with keys on his belt. He abandoned that image when he bought the Lagoon, and now he limped mysteriously around the sidelines of the dance floor, supported by a rosewood cane and dressed in a white suit and Panama hat.

The regular boys were back at the bar in force now, completing transactions, dancing, snorting coke by the door. Hermes, one of the newer regulars, sported a winged cap and pranced from the bar to the pool table, drinking white wine and socializing fervently.

But it seemed these innocent and newly vindicated boys were threatened again, this time by punk rockers, new wavers, and kung fu disco enthusiasts, who confused the Lagoon's penchant for gays with a general tolerance for the new or trendy. Consequently, the new punk regular was an anorexic blond who endured spiked heels, sweaty purple silk pants, a trench coat, and hair covering the left side of her face. She walked the dance floor, striking poses or examining herself in the new mirror lining the back wall.

Le Blanc seemed unwilling to subject himself to the rigors of the frenetic pace, relentless transactions and unpredictable evolution of the Blue Lagoon. In the past, when I worked in the office at Sweetwater Music and the Blue Lagoon needed pool cues or repairs on the *Amazon* pinball, Le Blanc and the other street mechanics would force Hans to make the trip. I wondered what plagued them, if they feared for their fragile psyches or their tender respectability. I wondered if the fear came from stereotypes or experience. I asked Le Blanc if anyone had ever harassed him there, if anything had ever gone wrong, but I was dismissed with indecipherable grumblings, designed to exhibit my impertinence.

That evening, the bouncer, Dante, greeted us at the door. He was an aging, convivial antique dealer who thrived on the evening's activities but couldn't reconcile his visits if he weren't working. Sitting at the door, he needn't drink or dance, but these pleasures were still within reach.

"The Duke is dead!" Dante announced as we walked up. I threw my arms around his 280-pound frame and gave him a kiss. He thanked me. Up this close, I could see that he had been crying. Dante stamped our hands with bright fuchsia lips, so that we could get back in later. Le Blanc inspected the lips on the back of his hand, while I told him his brand wouldn't come out for three days.

"Some bouncer," he said. "Who's the duke?"

"The Duke, oh, the Duke is Dead!!" Dante moaned, homing in on us at the pool table, the fuchsia kisser stamp still clutched in his fingers. "The Duke! John Wayne! You don't know who John Wayne is?"

Le Blanc was noticeably shaken to see this enormous elderly man carrying a stamp of fuchsia-inked lips and weeping over the death of John Wayne. Le Blanc's shoulders started to twitch. He just stood there stunned, the hand talc and cue chalk stacked up in his hands. I poked him alert, and then led Dante back to his post. When I returned to the pool table, Le Blanc asked me incredulously, "John Wayne wasn't gay, was he?" I said no. Le Blanc seemed to shudder, torn between compassion for Dante's grieving and revulsion at it. Or perhaps he shuddered thinking that an icon of masculinity like the Duke could be defiled by such an ardent display of good-intentioned but unconventional lust. Then he started to laugh. "Could tarnish a reputation," he said, and winked at me. He went over to the bar to collect the money for the talc and chalk.

I scrutinized the scene. Hermes was flitting between the dance floor and the bar, sipping the house white wine. The bartender was droning to him in his endless falsetto.

The punk and kung fu addicts had just gotten off work and were making their way toward the mirrored dance floor.

Brent, the owner, sat on a stool by the dance floor exit, dressed in his white three-piece suit and Panama hat, his cane straddling his knees. When he saw Le Blanc approach the bar he got up and went over to him, reaching his hand in his pocket, I assumed for some money. But shouldn't the bartender pay him out of the Lagoon's money for the pool table supplies, not Brent out of his own pocket? Then I thought about the "bank" that had kept coming up all day. The helicopter crash had made me forget about it.

While I was watching the transaction, Larry, an old high school friend of mine, appeared and prevented me from seeing exactly how much money was exchanged. He wanted news of a mutual friend, but when Le Blanc returned he looked skeptical, as if he suspected Larry of using me as a front for scoping out the new men. Larry was dressed in a G-string and knee-high leather fringe. Le Blanc said the *Amazon* pinball was busted, and he needed a score drum coil from the truck. I offered to get it myself, but he insisted and left. By the time he returned with the coil, Larry had retreated to the bar. Le Blanc displayed his fuchsia-lipped hand to get back in, replaced the coil, and insisted we go. I promised Dante I would come back the next night. Outside, Le Blanc heaved a sigh.

"Nothing happened," I said, in a way that was meant to be comforting, but sounded annoyingly glib.

"You feel so at home in that place," he said.

I knew he was thinking about all the other places we'd been to that day, where I didn't feel at home. "What are you so wigged out about?" I said.

We got in the truck; Le Blanc gripped the steering wheel with both hands and looked over at me. He looked like he was about to embellish Dante's perverted grief to me, and detail the treachery of Larry's G-string, but all he said was, "I just hadn't realized John Wayne died—that's all. It caught me off guard."

"Did they ask you about the bank in there?" I said.

He drove out of the parking lot. "Forget the bank," he said. Then he smiled and looked over at me. "Vassar. Cultural Anthropology."

"That's right," I said.

"So what are you doing driving a truck?" he asked.

"I told you, I wanted to come home."

"Before graduate school?" he said. I looked at him. "Don't worry. I won't get you fired. You're taking a year off before graduate school?" I told him I wasn't sure. I had things to think about. "You've applied for grants and fellowships, and grad schools, and you're waiting to hear."

"How do you know about this stuff?" I asked him.

"I don't," he said. "What's your specialty?"

"Ancient cultures," I told him.

"Etruscans, Babylonians, Greeks," he said.

"Hey, how do you know about this stuff?"

"So you may go to Greece next year, on some archae-ological dig?"

I didn't answer. Le Blanc called in on the radio to get the new repair calls. The answering service that fielded the calls at night told him the lady at Harvey's had retrieved her keys from the *Indy 500* at the bowling alley, and nobody else had called. So we were free until another machine broke down. We had caught up already.

Le Blanc racked up the radio microphone and turned left, toward the beach. "Where are we going?" I said.

"Your place?" he said. "You can show me your pottery chips, flint heads, arrows, and rare icons." I smirked at him. "Well how about dinner then?" I said I was hungry. Le Blanc turned around and went the other way.

"Now you know what I'm up to," I said. He told me again that I shouldn't worry, he wasn't going to spill the beans or anything. He just thought it was funny that I assumed he was some pinball flunkey who didn't know anything about Etruscans or Babylonians.

"Not a lot of people know about Etruscans," I said. "But that's not the point."

"So what's the point?" he said.

"The point is," I said, "since you know what I'm up to, why don't you tell me about the 'bank'? That's a fair deal."

"Forget about the bank," he repeated. I asked him if Brent, the owner of the Blue Lagoon, had made some "bank transaction" with him up at the bar. Le Blanc looked over at me and shook his head. "You know, you're right," he said, "nothing really happened at the Blue Lagoon." He laughed to himself.

I guessed he was right. Nothing much ever did happen there. It was riddled with possibilities—possibilities for drama, danger, and lust, but all that materialized were a few one-night stands, some posing, interesting costumes, and cocaine. As we pulled into the parking lot of an all-night diner, Le Blanc mumbled something about the Blue Lagoon representing the seamy underbelly of American life. I said it was a safe place to dance.

CHAPTER TWO

Pageant

When Le Blanc and I started out on the route the next morning it had been raining for several hours; the streets were already starting to overflow. Sweetwater County had a tendency to flood easily when it rained, but residents approached the hardship with both whimsy and caution, kayaking through the streets to work when the water level got high enough and sandbagging the beaches at the first sign of danger. I figured hydroplaning along the roads in the truck and wading into the clients' establishments with soggy cigarettes wasn't going to make my training any easier, but I had to keep the problem in perspective the way the rest of the locals did. After all, flooding was one of our few problems, besides tourists and serial killers.

Le Blanc and I were quiet on the ride over to Electronex, our first location. He didn't mention the helicopter crash or my bachelor's degree in Cultural Anthropology from Vassar; I didn't mention his homophobia, my theory on the socioeconomic correlates to preference for certain cigarette brands or the elusive bank that all our clients kept mentioning. But I had stayed up all night thinking about it, and I was beginning to get an idea what it might mean.

Le Blanc introduced me to B.F. Manta, the guard at Electronex. B.F. was so delighted at having a new cigarette driver in his domain that he dressed us up in those dust-proof uniforms (white mylar jumpsuit, neck cover and gathered bonnet) and took us for a tour of the facilities.

He donned his own dust-proof regalia, attaching the neck cover with great care, and told us, rubbing his mylar glove against the dust-free wall of the first Clean Room, that today's rain was deceptive, that really the earth was becoming dryer and dryer, creating more deserts, which was exactly what cancer was doing to the body. It was the desertification of the body, the drying out of each cell until the body died.

B.F. Manta looked like a Palm Springs golfer. He had a thick, enforced tan, which I could see through the mylar jumpsuit. He wore a shiny gray toupée that was reflecting light onto the dust-free ceiling. His eyes were an unavoidable aquamarine color, which reminded me of the over-chlorinated motel pools in the desert. Maybe it was just the strong smell of chemicals in the dust-free area. We were pausing over a vat of something, and the fumes grazed my face.

I asked what the vat was, and if it was heating, since an iridescent shine emanated from it. Or perhaps it was a fluorescent light. It was attached to a computer whose pink buttons flashed on and off. "Cosmic, isn't it?" B.F. Manta remarked, instead of answering my questions. He went on to say that Cosmic was in *Star Wars*, *Close Encounters*, and the *Star Trek* revival. I asked him about the vat again. He said that there were even some clips in that month's *Playboy* of some guy getting jerked off by a UFO playmate. The playmate was metallic blue, with pop eyes and no hair. She was shaped and textured like a Barbie doll, milky and plastic.

He rubbed his hand on the arm of my mylar dust-free suit as an example. Le Blanc raised his eyebrows at me from underneath his bonnet. I browsed the room, turning on sinks, welders, and gas outlets, and inspecting shiny discs that reflected rainbow colors, chevron patterns, or multicolored grid formations depending on how I held them up to the light. I stood at the window and looked into the next room. There was heavy equipment in it. I inspected the workers in their dust-free costumes, peering under the bonnets, trying to ascertain what kind of cigarettes they would smoke.

B.F. Manta went on to tell us that the couple was positioned on a glass bed that was lit from underneath, fluorescent colors glittering in the background. She turned into a human, seduced him and vanished. "Now that's what I call an interplanetary relationship," B.F. said.

I asked to see the heavy machinery and he took us in the next room. He pointed to the switches we mustn't touch. I got down on my hands and knees and tried to look underneath. One piece of equipment was a giant pipe laid on its side, with glass ends and smaller glass tubes running through the middle.

B.F. Manta insisted that we were turning away from catastrophe thrillers and turning to space thrillers—suspense and gore transformed into Cosmic musing. He patted the cylinder approvingly and I asked him to explain what was inside. He peered into it with me, and said it was a giant X-ray machine of some sort, like a telescope. Le Blanc shrugged.

As he led us out into the hallway and helped us take our bonnets off, B.F. said that people liked the idea of what could be possible. "Entertainment to take the strain off the work week."

It was 7am and the graveyard shift was letting out. Le Blanc thanked B.F. and led me into the cafeteria, where the cigarette machines were located.

"Is that guy for real?" I asked Le Blanc while I got the hang of where to kick the door and which way to rattle it in order to open the first cigarette machine.

"The Cosmic Communion," Le Blanc said. "It's always been B.F.'s private obsession."

"Come on," I said, figuring he was making another joke at my expense.

"Serious," he said. "B.F. would do just about anything to have his own UFO playmate, his own extraterrestrial to sleep with."

"Give me a break," I said. Le Blanc just shrugged and showed me how the cigarette machines were laid out, where the counters and running tallies were located in each machine, how the distribution was set up. These electronics workers were mainly Marlboro-box smokers, in short, the middle classes, with some long and light cigarettes, some Winstons and some oddball brands thrown in to make it look open-minded.

As I was filling the machines and practicing my carton slicing and pack stacking techniques, Le Blanc launched into a veritable sermon about B.F., how he was always like that, very chatty, relentlessly on-the-make, and would hold me up for hours with tours and discourses on various galactic perversions if I didn't treat him brusquely. I just shook my head. "No he won't," I said.

Le Blanc started laughing. When I asked him what his problem was now, he said, "I can't believe I'm leaving you to fend for yourself among all these pimps, thieves, felons, swindlers and perverts."

"Oh spare me the soap," I said. "Put the violins away for Christ's sake."

He said, "Okay, okay," and threw up his hands like I was the one being ridiculous.

Alphonso's Penny Arcade

When we got outside again the rain was coming down so hard we could barely see through it. I was glad Le Blanc was driving. He headed down to the wharf, where we serviced an arcade that specialized in the old wooden games, like skeeball, which involved rolling a ball up a slope into holes. Alphonso, the arcade's owner and a Sweetwater native, had a large interest in the Sweetport Lumber Company and a larger interest in the Wharf's fisheries, but he was civic-minded, muleheaded and pugnacious, and insisted that the teenagers would not have any place from which to come in off the streets if Alphonso did not provide for them. When I had worked in the office, occasionally I heard the Arcade had been raided for illegal gambling or underage beer drinking, or Alphonso had been cited for harboring a runaway who was violating his probation, but usually the police left Alphonso alone. A year before, when his wooden foosball tables were cracking from salt corrosion and the skeeballs were splintering, Alphonso finally agreed to let Sweetwater Music buy his equipment, restore it and re-install it. He would take a percentage of the profits from the refurbished machines, once they were owned by Sweetwater Music.

But Alphonso never did anything without sufficient motive, and that time, Le Blanc did not suspect the extent of his evil genius. The true reason Alphonso sold was because he had harbored a passion for remodeling the arcade, but couldn't bear the hassle and expense of moving all his beloved machinery out. This way, unknown to Le Blanc, Alphonso could redecorate with no inconvenience, and have all his machinery come back good as new, for no cost. Alphonso's secret dream was about to come true.

So he kept the pleasure to himself, and the moment Sweetwater Music had removed the last aging pool table, Alphonso summoned the electricians, painters, carpenters, muralists, leaded glass craftsmen and carpet layers. When Le Blanc returned to re-install the machines, he found that the new carpets were so thick and bumpy he couldn't level the pool tables, the pinballs kept registering Tilt because they jolted so easily on the mushy surface, and the video games continually shorted out since the wall circuitry had been rewired incorrectly.

Alphonso was delighted; Le Blanc muddled through. Now, no matter how often Alphonso called to report a broken machine, Le Blanc only consented to repair them when he came in to collect the money from the games.

When we arrived at the Arcade that morning, troops had already come out from Fort Emeryville to sandbag the beaches. Le Blanc had been navigating his truck with limited success over the flood-gutted streets. The community had dragged out its surfboards, boogie boards, dinghies, canoes, inflatable rafts, and lifeboats, and was commuting rather happily that way. A lot of people were down at the beach, helping out the military.

Inside the Arcade, Alphonso told us that by early that morning water had soaked into the carpets and the machinery had started toppling. By the time we arrived, the pool table greens were soggy and the flood had turned the pinballs on their heads. Alphonso was in his favorite pair of waders, usually reserved for when the steelhead were running. I began to use the pool cues to fish small objects out of the soup. Some of Alphonso's more gallant young customers had arrived in full wetsuits to recover the treasured pool balls, but the boys were mostly a nuisance, knocking into Alphonso while he was trying to fish and disturbing the equipment that was still standing.

Le Blanc told me we had to figure out a way to get the machines upright and keep them up, so only the legs would be damaged, and not the machinery and circuitry inside. In a rare flash of insight, I collected all the large metal milkshake mixer glasses and tucked them under the legs of a *Jungle Rescue Squad* pinball. The volunteer frogmen held the machine upright while I performed the operation. The glasses were large enough to form air pockets, keeping the machine upright and afloat. When I was finished the entire crowd stood there and applauded, even Le Blanc. It was my moment of glory. I was beginning to think I could hold my own in this business after all.

While we were securing the other machines I noticed one of the frogmen looked familiar. He was that blond kid Kenny Sears, who surfed near my apartment, and whom I had seen in the holding tank at the jail the day before.

"They let you out?" I said to him. He blushed and swatted his hand at me. "Are you okay?" I asked him. The other boys in wetsuits began to stop what they were doing and turn around to listen. Kenny Sears was something of their idol, since he was the best surfer in town.

"Yeah, yeah," he said, "forget it," and finished propping up the *Invaders From Mars* pinball machine.

When Le Blanc and I had finished securing the equipment, we filled the cigarette machine with Marlboros and rushed back to the truck. "So you prefer blonds," he said as we were running over. I didn't know what he meant, so I just shrugged at him. He unlocked the truck.

The rain seemed to be abating. Le Blanc said it was time to eat some breakfast and dry off. He drove us over to the Sweetwater Hotel and led me inside.

We entered through the bar, and Le Blanc pointed out the cigarette machine. "That's yours," he said, "there's another by the cashier's counter." We sat in the back dining room that was decorated in red velveteen like an old movie house, with red vinyl booths along the walls and black tables with red chairs in the center. The red wallpaper was flocked with a fleur-de-lys design, like a bordello, and there were pictures of girls in chiffons, wearing crowns and holding scepters, hung on all the walls. Le Blanc caught me looking at them.

"Haven't you ever seen the Miss California photos before?" he asked me. I told him I'd only eaten in the front dining room. "They start over there," he said, pointing to the door, "from 1947, and come around here to the present."

I got up to look more closely. Le Blanc wasn't kidding. There they were, all the Miss Californias since 1947, strung out in order above every table, starting from the door of the dining room, passing the door to the kitchen and extending all the way to the bar entrance—Beauties starting in black and white, passing through a greenish tinted color phase, and emerging in brilliant Technicolor. Le Blanc lounged in the booth while I browsed, and after he figured I had fogged up the glass of enough photo frames he disengaged himself from the vinyl, took me gently by the wrist and led me over to the glass case where the crown and scepter were displayed.

What an astonished, precious and rarified world this Hotel dining room was. Filled with Beauties and zircons! The back and bottom of the case were padded with silk; the wand itself was leaning up inside, a diagonal of magic. The crown lay at the bottom of the case. It too was covered with zircons studded here and there with a red garnet.

Aghast and ablaze with this mania, I slumped into our booth. I had never really thought about the ramifications of the Miss California Pageants I had seen as a child: the 49th state of the Union playing queens and Thunderbirds. Chiffons and elbow gloves! A whole state converged on Sweetwater for the sake of wands. A wand convention directed by the Beauties. The pressure of it was too much. Le Blanc told me I was just traumatized by the monsoon and the scuba diving at Alphonso's Arcade, and made me drink some hot coffee. He ordered me a full breakfast, steak and eggs with a side order of buckwheat pancakes and two glasses of milk, and then he asked me why I was so attracted to that surfer Kenny Sears.

"Excuse me?" I said.

He told me I was young enough to go out with the guy; after all, high school and college weren't that far apart, and as a detached observer, since he was old enough to be my father, he was just wondering what the appeal was, of a kid like that. I just shook my head and didn't answer him. Then the eggs and pancakes came.

Okay, so none of us were immune. We all had our quirks, idiosyncrasies, preoccupations. I had a fondness for teenage boys, especially blonds. I liked to watch them play pinball and surf. I liked to watch them because they were angel-faced and clear-eyed, they never walked their boards down to the water. I liked them because they looked so serious while their hair was always messed up and because they had no idea how sleek and graceful they looked, balancing and paddling. They embodied the best of both sexes, agile and sturdy, intense and careless.

After all, when I returned to Sweetwater after college, I didn't move back in with my parents; I took a studio down at the beach, and I started watching them surf. I began to wonder, why was it that surfers were blond and never walked from their bicycles to the waves? Each boy tucked his board under his arm and ran barefoot, booties flapping against his thighs. Was the tide going to change?

I did not pay much attention to them at first. I frequented the Bluff only to relax after work, to be outside after an entire day in the Sweetwater Music office. But after a few weeks I began to thrive on their dancing.

Of course there was one boy who did it best. He was skinny and blond, with a chiseled face and green eyes. He paddled out the farthest, turned his board against the wall of water in one deft steer and traveled it, inside and on top, twirling the board in circles, himself the other way. As the wave careened and wound down he taunted it, trying to provoke it into throwing him off. Sure, he could jump onto a wave, race and weave, but the defiance was in the dancing.

The Bluff was the legendary surfing spot in Sweetwater, an expanse of cliff that cut a series of waves all along it, the tallest at the cutting edge and the beginner's waves at the length of the cliff where it wound down to the Wharf. The Annual Surfing Championships were held at the Bluff every December. Kenny Sears always won. He was the best surfer in town.

I had tried to learn how to surf in order to meet him. This romance cost me a fractured skull. I enrolled in a weekend physical education class at Sweetwater High Adult School. I had trouble maneuvering into the school bus clad in my damp wetsuit. We drove to the beginner's spot by the wharf. I couldn't manage staying on my board even on my belly, grew fatigued just paddling out. My upper arms locked in an up-swinging position. The waves rolled right over me.

With a supportive war cry the instructor gave me a push and I caught one. I made it to my knees. Heady with success I tried to stand. On my way up I lost my balance and kicked the board out from under me. The board boomeranged, smacking me just below the eye. The results were a concussion, blow out fracture of the left orbital, and a reprimand from the grocer: Whoever he is, he's not worth that black eye.

I should have showed Kenny my surfing injuries, or persisted in learning, but instead I waited until the eye healed and became a spectator again. One day, as he was walking to his red Sprite sports car, I slipped a note under his windshield wiper and drove off in my own brown Austin. Kenny was curious; he chased my car until I had parked and he had seen where I lived. He came over one day on his skateboard and stood at my door for a while talking to me, but he wouldn't come in and I forgot to ask his name. He avoided me after that. I tried leaving him a note to meet me at the Blue Lagoon. He showed up, but he played pool and left without talking to me. I hadn't seen him since, until the day before, when he turned up in the holding tank of the Jail.

Le Blanc and I had finished eating breakfast. I pushed my plate away and looked up. Brent, the owner of the Blue Lagoon, was standing at the entrance to the dining room in his white suit and Panama hat, admiring the early photos of the Miss California winners.

"I'm sorry," Le Blanc said, "I didn't mean to dredge up unpleasant memories, I was just curious, as a casual observer." I swore at him and got up. He laughed, and told me he'd never seen me so touchy about anything before. I went over to Brent and introduced myself as the new cigarette driver for Sweetwater Music. We admired the photographs together while Le Blanc paid the bill. I was tempted to ask Brent what the bank was, or what he was doing up so early, in the same clothes he was wearing the night before, but I was too busy sulking, and didn't have the nerve to do either.

The rain stopped, the streets drained, and the rest of the day passed without incident. Le Blanc treated me gingerly, as if I were some mysterious creature whom he had inadvertently wronged.

When we got back to the shop, I counted the cigarette money by myself. In the warehouse, Tammy was complaining to Le Blanc and Hans that quality candy had gone from ten to thirteen cents wholesale, and HTZ had decided we could no longer vend it at twenty-five; instead he was buying six-cent candy and selling it at twenty-five, or trying. She said the six-cent candy tasted so bad it didn't move at all, it just sat in the machine and spoiled. Tammy insisted that the thirteen-cent candy would move twice as fast, incur no spoilage, bring in the same profit, and keep the customers happy in the good bars, but HTZ said no, he couldn't make a profit on thirteen-cent candy.

Le Blanc asked Tammy what the official word was on the Tax Man, and she said that HTZ announced the guy had found nothing, but the comptroller looked especially haggard that day, and Alice said he'd spent most of his time locked in his office with the curtains shut. Hans said it sounded like they were trying to clean things up before the Tax Man came back.

I went into the office to see what I could find out. HTZ was lurking around Alice's desk, watching the list of broken machines grow longer. He even tried to raise Chester on the radio but he wouldn't answer.

It didn't seem to be a good time to ask Alice about the comptroller. I tried to get a look at him, but the door and curtains were shut. I imagined him hunched over a dubious book entitled *Projected Earnings for October 1977*, pausing to sip his highball, a waft of hairstyling gel and expensive bourbon rising from his collar. He would be penning in the exact figures off the back sides of Chester and Le Blanc's music and games receipts, and Hans' on-call service receipts.

"I thought I made a rule that the street mechanic was to call in every hour. Didn't I make a rule?" HTZ said. When Chester finally did call in, HTZ tried to get on the radio to repeat the rule, but Alice didn't have time. Alice had her own ideas about the guys in the shop, and especially about male and female.

In past years Alice had been easygoing. Things could be what they were. But since HTZ took over she'd gone stubborn. Her instincts rebelled against the change. She felt he was bringing about destruction without our knowledge. To guard herself against him, to warn us that this change threatened, Alice had revoked her tolerance.

Things could no longer be what they were. Now they had to be female.

I had heard people talk of boats as female: *She's going under*, or *bring her around*. So at first I thought Alice had devised a system, candy machines and jukeboxes female, pool tables and pinballs male. I was wrong.

"WGFZ to Ace l9," Alice said, when she finally raised Chester, "I got a Rockola 442 juke at the Lazy Days Bar with a scratched Mel Tormé record on her."

"Any other calls?" Chester said.

"I've got a list longer than she's wide, so you just wait a minute. She's all clogged up again at the Guadalupe P.O."

"Has Hans been buying beet sugar for the coffee machines?" Chester asked.

"He knows she chokes up on beet sugar quicker than cane." Alice went through the rest of the list. Finally she paused.

"Is that all?" Chester said.

"She's all clear," Alice answered. Even the abstract slate emptied of Chester's service calls was female. Once, when Le Blanc had stayed out all night working and Maria came into the shop to make a scene, Alice helped him out. Maria blazed into the shop railing that Le Blanc had been to the Blue Lagoon, yearning for boys younger than his own sons. Boy-chasing being the ultimate insult to the men in our shop, Le Blanc was too indignant to defend himself.

"All babies are girls, pretty and unformed, half of them are just waiting to become something else—Men. That includes every child under seventeen, male or female. They're all girls," Alice had explained.

"And younger than his sons is too young to get into the Blue Lagoon," Tammy had advised, emphasizing the practical. "I wouldn't tear out my hair, honey, would you rather he'd been with me?" That put an abrupt end to the argument. It was the nicest remark Tammy had ever offered on behalf of a man. Maria went home furious, and no one received home-baked cookies from her that Friday.

I gave up on the idea of finding out about the comptroller and went out to the parking lot to help Le Blanc load the truck. But he was loading mine as well as his. He told me that at nine the next day I had to meet Tammy at the base of the mountains and go with her up to the Nuclear Missile Installation. She knew the layout up there better than he did, and would show me where the cigarette machines were located. In the afternoon I would be on my own. Then he apologized for asking me about Kenny at breakfast. "Forget it," I said. I asked him if Hans was all right after that helicopter crash the day before. He told me he seemed fine.

"If I thought it would upset you, I wouldn't have asked," he said. I told him again to forget it. "But now you'll never show me your arrows or flints or pieces of broken pottery," he said.

I laughed and took hold of his shoulder. "You can see those anytime," I said.

"Really?" he said. I nodded. "How about tonight after dinner?" I said it was fine with me, I mean, who was I to deny a grown man flints and arrows and pottery chips? He told me it was settled then and he would meet me at my place around eight.

When I arrived home, the sun was setting over the water like something out of a greeting card with the caption, *Wish you were here*. In any other town it would have been a quiet evening. People would have been arriving home from work, retrieving the newspaper off the lawn, greeting their families.

But not in Sweetwater—in Sweetwater the surf was up. Young couples crowded into dockside bars, ordered strawberry daiquiris and clamored for the "sundowner" tables where they could survey the action on shore. The Beautiful People rushed to the yacht harbor to prepare their boats for the Tuesday night sailing regatta. The bulk of the seaworthy population loaded their surfboards into their Woodys and vans, strapped their knee boards to the roofs of their Volkswagens, or simply tucked their boogie boards under their arms and jumped on their bicycles. They were headed for the Bluff.

Since Le Blanc wouldn't arrive until eight and it was only six-thirty, I decided to walk out to the Bluff for a while and watch the surfers, just to kill time. Okay, so I was kidding myself. I went anyway. I started at the southern end of the cliff, closest to the wharf, where the waves were the smallest and the learners cast out tentatively on their long boards. Most of these beginners were young boys aged seven to ten, eager to infringe upon their older brothers' domain further up along the cliff. An older woman walking her Pekinese stopped here to watch a beginner slide his long board down the treacherous cliff face to the water below. A skater also stopped to adjust her fluorescent striped knee socks before starting out again along the walkway that followed the Bluff as far north as the lighthouse. A tourist snapped a photo of the wharf across the cove.

I walked up toward the lighthouse, dodging skaters and obsequious dogs. While I was walking, cars backed up all along the route. Some drivers waited for surfers ahead of them to pull over and park their vans. Others stopped to talk to friends who had already parked and were changing into wetsuits behind their open car doors. One guy stopped and let a surfer riding shotgun jump out, run to the cliff's edge, gauge the size of the swell and run back to make his report. Spectators from the cliffs and wet surfers taking a rest ran out into the street to talk to friends stuck in traffic. One wet surfer accepted a beer from the passengers in the back of a Chevy Malibu. He invited them to a party that would be held later on that evening, when the tide was low. At the pickup truck behind them, phone numbers were exchanged.

The elite congregated at the high end of the Bluff near the lighthouse, where the waves were the largest and only the best surfers showed off their talent. When I reached this spot I saw Nick Tatum, a burly, overcooked fellow in his sixties, who had been one of the original surfers in Sweetwater. As a teenager he had made a pilgrimage to the North Shore of Oahu and had come back invested with a mission: to cultivate Sweetwater into the mainland surfing Mecca. He had driven himself to become the best surfer around, and had shown surfing movies at the public library on Thursday nights. Eventually, with the help of family financial backing, he had produced a line of Tatum surfboards that were featured at that winter's North Shore Surfing Tournament. Tatum lost his eye in a wipeout in that tournament, an accident that secured his dream. Sweetwater surfing and Tatum boards became legendary. The Beach Boys started singing about them. In the next ten years, Nick Tatum would have boogie boards, knee-boards, short boards, wetsuits and surf wear all bearing his name. Even after he became famous, Nick Tatum stayed in Sweetwater. He was one of the local celebrities. And Sweetwater had become the surfing Mecca he had dreamed of, with Tatum himself as the prime architect.

I stood conspicuously by a payphone and watched the boys come up to Nick, shake his hand, and show him the dings and dents in their surfboards. They pointed out to sea when they spoke to him, recounting their treks up and down the coast where they had been surfing recently—re-enacting the conditions, the great rides. The proudest boys even had shark teeth imbedded in their boards from dangerous forays as far south as Point Lobos and as far north as Half Moon Bay. These brave ones stood with Nick at the Bluff and watched their friends ride. Sometimes they talked about the swell or the break, or different rides they had seen that day, but mostly they talked equipment. The boys loved to talk equipment with Nick. They had grown up with his name plastered on their skateboards and flashed across their surfing magazines. Nick Tatum *was* equipment.

By now I had spotted Kenny's car in the Lighthouse Point parking lot, and I had located him in the water, so I was dividing my spectator time between the show on land and the show at sea. To some people, "making the scene" was more interesting than the scene itself. But to me Kenny's surfing seemed much more intriguing. If he had been on land, perhaps I would have felt differently.

I was obliged to give up my post, however, because someone wanted to use the pay phone, and when I did so I lost sight of Kenny in the water. He was easy to find, no one turned his board to catch a wave in one deft motion the way he did, or spun and twirled as adroitly on the board, but he had disappeared. So I took up a new station along the wooden railing and went back to watching Tatum. He had gathered quite a group around him, and had knelt down to examine the heel of one boy's bootie.

Just then the tip of Kenny's short board appeared on the stairway up the cliff and Kenny underneath it. The crowd of boys parted for him and he greeted Nick. Nick wanted to know how the new equipment was working out. Since Kenny was the best surfer in Sweetwater, he had earned the right to advertise the new boards and wetsuits by trying them out in the water. This heightened his fame and expertise to the other boys, who longed for the sharpest wetsuits and fastest boards, but couldn't talk their mothers into buying them.

Kenny unzipped the top of his suit, flicked back his long blond hair in one elaborate motion, the way an anxious horse or a vain girl might do, and stood there patiently while Nick examined his seams and the other boys tried to run their hands along his new board. I turned to go, but he had already seen me. Kenny always drew a crowd, and I always seemed to be stationed a little ways off from it, watching.

I took my time walking home. When I opened the door to my apartment, a note fell down from where it had been wedged just above the doorknob. I figured I had missed Le Blanc, but the note said *Sorry about the Jail—KS.* I was about to go inside but Le Blanc pulled up, so I went to the corner to greet him. That's when I saw

Kenny's Sprite, just out of view around the side of the building. When he saw me he revved the engine and screeched around the corner past Le Blanc's truck. Le Blanc turned to watch him go by.

"You just can't get enough of that guy, can you," Le Blanc said.

"Oh please," I said. I showed him the note.

He said the boy was a true gentleman and bowed toward the door, insisting I go in first. He followed me through the kitchen into the main room. "I guess these beach places aren't very big," he said.

I asked him if he had eaten and he said he had. I asked him if he was backed up on calls and he said Hans had agreed to take them for the evening. I was pleased but uneasy, the way a person feels when he gets what he wants sooner than he expected.

"Do you want a drink?" I said.

He looked back at the kitchen. He said he wanted what he came for, and after a calculated pause added, "I want to see the flints, the arrows, the pottery chips…" He held out his hands in a beseeching manner.

"I'll get you a beer first," I said. "It'll soften the blow."

He shrugged and told me he would indulge my whim this one time. When I brought him his beer I found him examining the books on the shelf above my desk, taking some out to thumb through the pages.

"Well?" he said.

I opened a closet where I kept racks of samples. It was memorabilia for the most part, like a child's collection: sand and shells, rock samples, with a few replicas and real specimens thrown in.

He lit his pipe and turned the pieces over in his hands one by one, like a scholar or a voluptuary might. "It's amazing what kinds of civilizations they built," he said. "Thousands of years before Christ." He returned a jar of sand to the shelf and looked at me. "The Minoans in particular. Have you been to Crete?"

I retreated to the kitchen, sat down at the table with a beer, and tried to blow notes down the narrow neck, the way my father had taught me. Le Blanc followed me in.

"Did I say the wrong thing?" he said. "More bad memories?"

"Le Blanc, I have to tell you something," I said.

"Please. No confessions."

"No, it's not like that. It's nice. Well, sort of. Remember in the truck, on the way back to the shop yesterday, you told me I thought you were some pinball flunkey who didn't know anything?"

"Oh, forget that," he said. "Come on inside, bring your beer. Let's sift through the rest of the ruins."

I told him I felt really bad about that. I mean, maybe I felt that way but I really hadn't thought about it one way or another. I just didn't think. And there he was, training me when I was just going to leave in a year.

Le Blanc stood up and pulled me up by the arm. "Are you finished?" he said. I nodded. Then he told me he didn't want my sympathy. I told him I was trying to apologize; I wasn't trying to patronize him. But everything came out wrong.

He shook me by the shoulders. "Hey," he said. "You haven't drunk your beer." I looked down at it. He lifted my chin up with his hand, very gently, the way they do it in the movies, and he kissed me. "You should drink bourbon," he said. "It would make you alluring." He put his arm around me and led me out into the main room. He sat me down on the bed and held his hand up to my face. He looked at me with that same absorbed voluptuary's look he had given the sand and pottery chips. I asked him how he'd gotten interested in the Minoans, but he was leaning over to kiss me again. I noticed he wore a chain around his neck, hidden under his shirt, and I wondered what was at the end of it.

Tammy on Men

At nine the next morning I met Tammy on Jensen Creek Road. She told me she'd volunteered to take a ride with me up to the Nuclear Missile Base because Le Blanc didn't know how to navigate the mountain road, or drive by the armory without setting the missiles off. She usually met her kids at the mobile home for lunch, but she'd told her son to keep his sisters in the house at all costs, and given him permission to feed them frozen dinners and let them watch cartoons if necessary.

On Jensen Creek Road, she explained that her husband used to be a sawmill guard, holed up thirty miles from any town on a windy, treacherous road. She said she learned to drive on that road, trying to reach town to avoid going stir crazy, so this Creek Road never bothered her. I asked her what her husband did now. "That one? Hell, he left years ago, honey," she said.

At the gate Tammy introduced me to the guard and told him I would be servicing the cigarette machines. When we drove on I asked her how many kids she had in the mobile home. She said she had the one son from the mill guard, and three daughters from a beer truck driver who ran off with her best friend when she was pregnant with her last daughter. When she went in the office for a minute I stayed behind in the truck and tried on her butterfly frame glasses. They were nice—very Fifties, with zircons at the tips. When she came out again I asked her where she was from. "Born in Oklahoma, bred in Tennessee," was her answer.

She showed me how to drive by the armory without setting the missiles off. It was simple really; you just had to turn your CB radio off before you got within a certain range. And there were signs everywhere telling you NO RADIOS BEYOND THIS POINT. I suspected it was more to avoid eavesdropping than detonation. In the lake near the armory some of the nuclear engineers were going for their lunchtime swim, which Tammy said they did most workdays. I wondered out loud if they could get radiation that way. "Ugliest sight there is, a man without no clothes on," she said.

In the cafeteria I watched her fill the cigarette machine so I would know how to do it next time. As she was counting the packs, her thumb, which was resting on the open machine door, dropped enough to graze the inside wires of the selector buttons and shock her. She swore. In an insufficient attempt to console her, I asked if she had burned herself badly. "Only thing ever burned me is a MALE," she said.

Through a series of misalliances, errors in judgment and an irreverence for male pride, Tammy had embraced a passionate loathing for the male gender. I didn't pay much attention to her remarks at first; I figured her constant badmouthing of the guys at the shop was just her way of being sociable. But I was beginning to realize that almost no one of the male gender was exempt. Le Blanc seemed to be the only man I'd ever seen her treat kindly.

A man in the cafeteria asked Tammy to put more peanut clusters in the candy machine. Tammy obliged him, and while she was doing it the guy told her she looked familiar. "I fill those food machines every Monday," she told him. But the guy said no, she looked more familiar than that, she looked like one of the girls who came up on the weekends to swim in their lake.

Tammy scowled at him and we went back to the truck. On the drive down the mountain, she told me that when the locals had found out there were good swimming lakes up on the Nuke Base property, they started sneaking in at night and on weekends to swim naked. Everyone had a lot of fun and tried to keep it safe and quiet. But she had heard that lately some local entrepreneur had made it into a business. This mercenary was paying the guard and had even hired a lifeguard. The locals were so fond of their swimming hole they paid for the service, so the operator was making a profit. She asked me if I'd tried it and I told her no. She said that I should bring Le Blanc up and try it some time, that it was fun.

I looked at her to see if she knew about the night before, but judging by her expression the remark seemed innocent enough. She caught me looking at her.

"I know what you must be thinking," she said and lit up a Chesterfield. "That I'm pushing him off on you. Well, maybe I am, in a way." She tamped her cigarette ashes into the tray, and looked at me again. "He hasn't told you, has he," she said.

"Told me what?" I rummaged through the things we had discussed the night before and didn't find anything so portentous.

"Scott, the youngest son, the one he was supposed to have had with his current wife, Maria. The boy isn't even his. And I'll be damned if anyone knows who she's been having an affair with for the last ten years."

"I thought it was his first wife who cheated on him," I said.

"That one did too," Tammy said. She rubbed out her Chesterfield and lit another one. "Betrayed twice. Unusual for a man."

I examined the manzanita and pines going by. So that was why Le Blanc was the only man she approved of—he had been betrayed twice. "Does everybody know?" I asked.

"Nobody acts like they do," Tammy said. "Le Blanc will say a thing or two when he's had too much to drink, but you can't ever talk to him about it after that. Those are the rules."

When Tammy dropped me off at my truck on the bottom of Jensen Creek Road, I was thinking about Le Blanc's rules. Tammy reached across me and opened the door. I got out and thanked her for the Nuke Base tour. "You can't blame me," she said, "Can you?"

My first afternoon working my route alone was hardly without incident. At Electronex, I was chatting with one of the engineers there about B.F. Manta's UFO playmate when he told me that someone had hired B.F. to contract his own extraterrestrial. She dished out the Cosmic

Communion, for a fee, to any earth-bound electronics assembler willing to pay. Collecting the money from the workers, B.F. played pimp to his UFO, letting the workers pass into the back room at Electronex where they indulged in her.

At the Jail the sheriffs were admirably brief with me and did not torment me by holding me in any of the transition cages. Davey was starting his shift and the Panty Litany was being waged full blast. But this time panties did appear: blue, lace, pink, even stretch cotton. Before, the Panty Litany had seemed like a harmless outpouring of depravity. Now someone had transformed it into a thriving business.

"This is the last batch," Davey warned the inmates. "I'm not gonna get anymore."

For each panty a cellmate paid Davey a cigarette pack serving as a wallet, jammed with twenty-dollar bills.

Since the inmates were being supplied with panties that day, I was spared a second Litany and instead was treated to a confidential talk.

"Hey, psst. Cigarette Lady. Over here." I went over, always the sucker. "Have you been in the women's cellblock?" they wanted to know. I hadn't, no cigarette machines in there. I told them so. They proceeded to tell me how it was. "Not so bad really, there's room to walk around and the women don't beat on each other much," they said. "Not a whole lot to worry about if you're not gonna be there for a long time. You only gotta watch out for them ladies they throw in there when Detox gets too crowded. The Detox overload can get out of hand. Know what I mean?"

Sure, I nodded. I had no idea what they meant. On the way out I asked Davey what these panties were all about, and if I could buy some from him. He shook his head and said that was the last batch he'd ever sell. He chewed on his toothpick. "I thought the guys in there just told you what was what," he said, "but if you still don't know, I'm not gonna be the one to tell you." He beat out a reggae tune on his knees. I wondered if those panties had diamonds or heroin or guns sewn inside the cotton crotch liners.

My last stop of the day was the B&B Card Room and I was anxious to get to it. I repeatedly tried to turn my truck down a side street to reach the shopping mall area where the card room was located, but every road was barricaded with City of Sweetwater wooden saw horses. I pulled over to find out what was happening. Sure, it was a balmy Monday in October, but some of us in Sweetwater resisted these enticements relentlessly luring us away from our salaried jobs.

There were sawhorses everywhere, all the way down to the beach on both sides of the street. I did not see how I could possibly get around them unless I drove to the top of town and tried to get through there. I entertained the idea that some political coup had divided Sweetwater in two. A cavalry rode by, the white horse's gear and riders chaps spangled with sequins. Spectators gathered and cheered. Police stood two abreast the City of Sweetwater sawhorses.

A string of go-carts followed the cavalry. Each cart had a sponsor's insignia emblazoned across its side: B&B Card Room, Oceansport Inn, Tommy's Burgers. Long-legged, hyperactive teenagers madly pedaled each cart. This display was also well guarded and vigorously cheered by the now hefty-sized crowd.

The climax of this part spectacle, part political coup, was a line of antique Thunderbirds, all of them white, impeccably waxed, tops down, each of them garnished by a girl. Not any girl, mind you, these were the Beauties themselves, long wavy hair topped by rhinestone crowns, girls clad in chiffon prom dresses and white gloves culminating at the elbow. The Beauties smiled, baring their teeth, and waved their wands to the now riotous crowd, which waved miniature official State of California flags back. Where did they get these flags, I wondered.

If this were a political coup I had come unprepared. Both sides were cheering. Suffering from a novel form of psychological sunstroke, I sat down on the lawn of the Civic Auditorium and tried to regroup myself while the crowd dispersed. Children dressed like Jack-in-the-Boxes trudged by on stilts. The sawhorses were collected on city trucks and carted away. I continued to the B&B Card Room.

The regulars at the B&B seemed oblivious to the change of regime that might have transpired outside and could threaten the very fiber of their lifestyle. Even though I feared rattling their poker games or provoking their dogs, I asked if they knew of the coup, if they had seen the horses, the militia two abreast, the Beauties waving wands. Apparently these Beauties were the Generals who had plotted the takeover and were now in control. I asked if they had seen the cavalry, the children on stilts.

The lifers said no. They were already used to me. B&B offered me a drink and I agreed to some strong coffee. He said all he knew was that the Miss California Pageant was held one week in October every year, starting with a parade on Monday and culminating with the crowding in the Civic Auditorium Sunday night. "Haven't you seen the photos and the crown and scepter in the Sweetwater Hotel Dining Room?" he asked me. I told him Le Blanc had shown me. "And was Brent there, the owner of the Blue Lagoon, looking at the pictures?" I asked him how he knew that. "You don't know?" he said and smiled ruefully. I asked him about the bank. "What bank?" he said.

That Nickel and Dime Stuff

On the way back to the shop, Alice reached me by radio and told me McKenzie's Pub in Emeryville needed cigarettes. MacKenzie's was supposed to have been my location, but Le Blanc had held onto it, insisting that it was easier for him to fill the cigarette machine when he serviced the pool table and that there was no point in me making a special trip all the way to Emeryville for one lousy machine. When he said this he was inside the shop, close by a wrecked coffee machine, and thumped the machine to emphasize the potential inconvenience.

Off the main drag, calculated to be just out of view of the Emeryville Shopping Mall, MacKenzie's Pub proved to be a chartreuse green stucco building capped by a white neon clover hung at strict right angles so it looked like a Nazi cross. This stucco madness had been erected in a vacant lot, now laced with mud ruts, the ruts deepened by the repeated tortures of pickups and jeeps. The minute I walked in the door I was facing the bar counter, which spanned the length of the opposite wall like a frontal attack. This head-on offensive left me uneasy; usually the bar counter was strung along a side wall.

To reach the bathroom you had to duck under this forbidding bar counter. Between the door and the bar lay the dance floor, almost wholly occupied by our cigarette machine, *Space Invaders* video and pool table, and carpeted with the spontaneous litter of peanut shells—preferred over the deliberate sprinkling of sawdust.

The barmaid, who introduced herself as Glenda, wore a garter and a cosmetically applied beauty mark on her cheek. Her customer at the bar wore a wide-brimmed cowboy hat and excruciatingly pointy red boots. Several seedy types slipped in, ducked straight under the bar to the bathroom, then exited a few minutes later. Then another beauty-marked, gartered barmaid emerged, also from the bathroom. I began to think that the bathroom was, after all, a backroom of some sort.

The cowboy at the bar pivoted his red pointy boot on the brass rail, turned to me, tipped his hat and said, "Yantree grows mulreys."

"Excuse me?" I said.

"Yantree grows mulreys," he repeated, and waved his hat at the cigarette machine.

I went over to the machine, opened it, and looked inside. Several rows were empty. "I'm sorry?" I said.

The cowboy slipped the napkin out from underneath his beer bottle, took a pen out of Glenda's apron and wrote something on it. He handed it to me. *WANT THREE ROWS MARLBOROS,* it said.

"There aren't enough columns of Marlboros, honey," Glenda explained. "They like the box type."

After I filled the machine and was getting ready to leave, I noticed that more customers were going in and out of the bathroom, barely stopping to buy a drink on the way. I knew no one was going to tell me anything, so I had to ask. Glenda told me that back there (pointing over her shoulder) was the bathroom for a nickel or dime, even for me. I laughed. "Only asking," I said. I turned to leave.

As I was walking out Glenda replied, "Sometimes asking is enough." I smiled and kept walking. "Maybe some other time," she said. When I reached the door she added, "It didn't use to be like this."

I nodded and left. When I was getting in my truck, I heard some glass breaking inside the bar. I was about to go back to see if she had hurt herself, but the noises stopped so I took off.

Simple Geometry

It was a muggy afternoon when I started back to the shop after MacKenzie's. I didn't know it yet, but Hans had been stumped by a rusty coffee machine and was fighting his worst instincts. He pulled on his Nordic God Thor anchor, as if he were trying to focus on his baby daughter, but instead kept imagining that he was a Sweetwater beach lifeguard again.

When Chester had come in for his lunchtime story, Hans had told him the one about the girl who kept pretending she was drowning because what she really wanted was for him to make love to her three miles out on his lifeguard surfboard. Since this story is a variation on "If she was hitchhiking then she was asking for it," Chester was annoyed, but kept quiet because it was humid out and Hans kept pulling on his anchor.

By the middle of the afternoon, Chester had returned again for parts, Le Blanc had come in to check some file information, and it was getting hotter outside. The conversation expanded from the lovemaking scene on the surfboard to other outdoor lovemaking experiences. Then it expanded from general lovemaking exotica to the recent *Playboy* Questionnaire: *Is it Nice to Have Sex with a Brussels Sprout?* Finally, the discussion fixed on hip-waist-breast measurements, the men talking late into the sultry afternoon, until bets were wagered and the question of who would buy several rounds of beer at the Guadalupe Hotel became contingent on a feature of my anatomy.

As yet, I knew nothing of this. After filling the cigarette machine at MacKenzie's, I called Alice on the truck radio to see if there were any other machines in Emeryville which needed filling. "She's all clear," Alice told me. But Hans got on the radio next.

"You got a tape measure in your truck, Maya?"

I asked him what for. I could hear scuffling noises in the radio. Perhaps HTZ was trying to get on the line from his Cadillac.

When I arrived at the shop they handed me the tape measure. Alice revealed to me later that they had drawn straws to see who had to go to the drugstore to buy it. I told them I was five foot ten, size nine shoes, size twelve clothes. They looked at each other. Hans volunteered the information.

"We've got three rounds of beer riding on your nipple diameter. I say two inches. Le Blanc says one and three quarters. Chester's going for one and a half." They explained to me that Chester was sure of himself because of his nudist club membership, Le Blanc because of his two marriages and Hans because of his work as a lifeguard.

I didn't know how to measure. Hans explained that it had to be right down the middle and drew me a circle complete with radius and diameter. "Simple Geometry," he said.

Hans won. Chester and Le Blanc would buy the beer. Alice was shaking her head, and announcing that the fellas never used to care about nipple diameter, when HTZ drove up, stormed into the warehouse and said he wanted to see everyone in the comptroller's office that very minute.

On the way in to the comptroller's office I asked Le Blanc what this could be about. "Maybe the Tax Man," he said.

The comptroller was seated at his desk with his hands folded in his lap, looking contrite, as if he had just committed a felony. HTZ was pacing behind him. His first order of business was to send Chester out on a service call. When that was done, HTZ told us that the nature of the business he had to discuss with us was very serious, that this was a team effort, that he needed our cooperation. Tammy shot a glance at Alice that looked like: *Since when has this been a team effort?*

HTZ went on to say that he not only needed our cooperation and our understanding but he needed us all to make sacrifices. Tammy looked over at Le Blanc this time as if to say, *I thought we were already making sacrifices.*

Then HTZ dropped the bomb. "Chester has been charged with child molesting," he told us. We all tried to look at each other—*Chester, the nudist with the sex therapist girlfriend?* "They're bringing the charges this evening, and he'll be out on bail in the morning." We stood there, nodding our heads, waiting for details, waiting for the sacrifice to be distributed among us.

"We have to show our solidarity for Chester," HTZ went on. "It's the only way to get him through this thing." I was wondering why HTZ didn't just cast Chester out and watch him sink. In other words, I was wondering what Chester could have on HTZ.

"So I've decided to promote Chester, make him the route manager. It's the only way to show we're behind him. Give him the best job in the company; give him responsibility. Le Blanc, you're the street mechanic from now on." Everyone looked at Le Blanc. He nodded. That was *his* sacrifice. I wondered what *we* were supposed to do.

Then HTZ went on to tell us that as we knew, the tax officials had been taking a look at the company records. Everything was in order, of course (or that's what he said), but HTZ wanted us to be extra careful not to make any mistakes in our receipts or calculations. Everyone nodded somberly as if this had extra meaning. I played along. Then HTZ said we knew what he meant, and issued a parting ultimatum, warning us that from then on our Christmas bonuses would be based on sales performance for the year, and would not be automatic as they had been in the past.

Back in the warehouse after the meeting, Tammy chain-smoked, Hans got up our orders, and the two of them kicked around various ideas concerning the details of Chester's demise, what the Tax Man had really found, and how they would buy Christmas presents for their children without bonuses.

I listened for a while, and then went looking for Le Blanc. I found him in the back of the shop, flushing out the tubes of a dying coffee machine and brooding over his new cuckold. Sure, it was necessary for Le Blanc to be demoted and Chester promoted. It lent Chester the credibility he needed for the trial. But the result on Le Blanc's side was always the same: jilted by a wife, a lover, a friend, and now his boss. Le Blanc had never thought well of himself, which only exacerbated this alternating fugue of sacrifice and betrayal.

"It's me, Maya," I said, bounding up behind Le Blanc as if I needed a formal introduction. "Can I buy you a beer at the Guadalupe Hotel?" I offered, hoping a binge would cheer him up.

"Would you drink bourbon?" he said.

The bar at the Guadalupe Hotel looked like the sleazy joint in a 1950s gangster film, where the hit man was supposed to meet his girl for the getaway, but of course she didn't show. Mainly, the bar was dark: the walls and wooden booths were dark, the floor was dark, the room was dimly lit. And in this darkness there shone beer signs. Above the men's restroom a mirrored beer sign reflected the customers' images back to them. Behind the bar another metallic beer sign picked up the glint of the liquor bottles and the bartender's watch. In the window, a neon beer sign was attacked by suicidal flies which had trapped themselves between the window and curtain. Beer signs even shone in the bottoms of the ashtrays when customers tamped their cigarettes.

We occupied the large corner booth where over the years various vilifications, slanders and obscenities had been tattooed into the wood in Spanish and Chinese. I imagined that an enterprising anthropologist could probably glean folklore and legend, several centuries of immigrant history, from these tables. The bartender was an enormous Chicano man named Isidro, who was so prepossessing in stature he had no need of a bouncer. He worked three jobs—mornings for the Sanitation Department collecting trash, daytimes repairing farm trucks at a nearby repair shop and evenings tending the Guadalupe Hotel Bar. He sent most of the money home to his mother and sister who, for some reason he had never revealed, could not or would not leave Mexico.

Tammy, Alice, Hans and Le Blanc all ordered different brands of beer. When Le Blanc brought the bottles to the table, and my coworkers each took one by the throat and twisted its cap off, it occurred to me that concomitant with the study of socioeconomic correlates to preference for certain cigarette brands, there was a heretofore uncharted world of beer brand preferences. Would the studies yield similar results? Would the groups divide along the same lines? I was curious to know, but figured that this cache of knowledge was the exclusive domain of beer truck drivers and bartenders.

Once we were settled in with our drinks, I just assumed we would talk about the events at hand—Chester's indictment and Le Blanc's demotion. I assumed that, in the supportive, self-conscious style of rhetoric bandied about during my college days, where victims were heroes to be praised vociferously and unrelentingly, everyone would offer condolences to Le Blanc, curse HTZ and worry out loud about Chester.

None of the above: Tammy noticed my bourbon and remarked that it was a new look for me. Alice asked me how the route went alone and chided Hans for sending me out on that MacKenzie's Pub call. She lamented again this newfound interest in nipple diameter, and asked Hans if he'd had any trouble on the repair route the night before. I thought the conversation would at least take a turn toward HTZ and end up with the Tax Man, but Hans and Tammy started talking about their children instead, and by then they had finished their beers. Le Blanc offered to corral another round, but Tammy insisted the Gang of Three had to go home, and Le Blanc should stay and sit with me while I nursed my bourbon and practiced my appeal.

At first I thought it was odd, or even coldblooded, that they hadn't said anything to Le Blanc. Then I realized they knew him better than I did. He had only just told me the night before that he didn't want any sympathy. To him it was demeaning, patronizing. They had respected his wishes and changed the subject.

Unfortunately, I was not as wise, not as mindful, and could not restrain myself. "Do you think Chester did it?" I asked after the others had left. Le Blanc waved me off, the way he would when I asked about the bank. I looked around at the cornucopia of dismal beer signs, twitching and flinching like faces. I had said the wrong thing again. Suddenly I became acutely aware of the stench in the bar, that acrid, moldy smell of stale cigarettes and vomit. I asked Le Blanc if we could leave, before I created a comic diversion.

CHAPTER THREE

Leveler

Things didn't change much in the next two months. Chester was official route manager, but Le Blanc ended up doing most of the work for him. Chester was preoccupied with the proceedings before the trial, which was to start the day after Christmas.

I had grown accustomed to my route, but the clients never seemed to get used to me. After Chester's indictment, all the expansive, good-natured cheer was gone. The proprietors looked at me suspiciously and asked me questions that I could not even understand, let alone answer. When I was discouraged and confused, I often stopped at the Sweetwater Hotel Dining Room to scan the walls of photos of the Miss California Pageant winners—the Beauties, as I called them. I often saw Brent there, the owner of the Blue Lagoon. He roamed the room in his white suit and Panama hat, his rosewood cane making clipping sounds on the polished dining room floor, and looked around wistfully, as if he had relinquished all promise, all future happiness in this room. He gave nothing away, but he wasn't suspicious toward me like the other clients. He treated me sympathetically, as if

I were experiencing rough times, which were not altogether my fault, but brought on perhaps by excessive zeal.

In my dogged, persistent way that had been thought charming with college professors, but was now infuriating, I kept pestering Le Blanc to spill the beans about the bank, Chester's indictment, anything he knew. I had seen a lot of Le Blanc during those two months, and eventually, one night when Le Blanc trusted me a little more, or was very drunk, he insisted it was his own fault Chester got in trouble, that he had unwittingly led Chester into a trap. He said HTZ could be turned belly-up at a moment's notice; Le Blanc, Chester and Hans would just have to get up the nerve to nail him. Le Blanc wasn't sure they had the nerve. I asked him what it all meant, but he wouldn't explain. He was scheduled to testify on the afternoon of New Year's Eve. The Annual Surfing Championships were set for that morning, and large crowds were expected to turn out for both events.

The good news was that around Thanksgiving, HTZ's wife had left him, taken the kids and filed for divorce. She was the object of sympathy around the shop, since HTZ propositioned every waitress in town and squandered a good portion of the company profits on his cocaine habit. We were convinced his wife would get more money out of him and certainly more peace by divorce. She was kind-hearted; she always said she didn't know what had changed him, but he was never like that before he bought the vending companies. The shop employees wanted to tell her, *Lust and Greed,* but we were shy and thought she was of a higher class than us because she was the boss' wife.

The comptroller reported that despite minor adjustments for the Tax Man, he could make the books balance just fine for 1977. In the past two months HTZ had purchased condominiums in Hawaii, motels in Emeryville and bowling alleys in Guadalupe. Judging by these acquisitions, we believed him. But nobody knew where the profits were coming from to finance this sweep of buying—or if they did, they weren't telling me. The money couldn't possibly have been coming from our diminished vending and games routes.

Now it was Christmas Eve. Tammy, Alice, Le Blanc and Hans were lingering in the lobby of the Oceansport Inn, watching me fill the cigarette machine. We didn't want to go inside the Ebb Tide Room to the company Christmas party, where the comptroller would hand out our Christmas bonus checks and HTZ would make a speech. Le Blanc's wife had refused to go to the party, and she was so mad she'd been asking everybody to quit their jobs. Le Blanc said he could start a hunting resort in Montana.

"My brother-in-law has offered to let me buy into his saw mill in Oregon," Hans countered. Tammy had no opportunities to leave town, so she didn't say anything.

We relented and went inside the Ebb Tide Room. The Oceansport Inn was not just another example of where Sweetwater had gone wrong. The Inn was the quintessential mistake, perhaps the seed of all ensuing mistakes. That night it seemed apt, a reminder of our own dilemma.

The Oceansport was the only high-rise in Sweetwater. Strategically located on the pivot point between the pier and the surfing grounds, the Inn drew customers and threw the favorite swimming cove into shadow for the entire afternoon. The love-hate relationship began there. Soon after its completion, the Oceansport Inn became the center of controversy over whether or not Sweetwater should be glamorized for the tourists, or whether its current charm should be preserved for the locals. The debate sifted down to economics, as most debates do. The developers claimed there would not be enough commerce without the proposed improvements.

The Oceansport Inn was the first in a proposed package of Inns, shopping malls, convention centers and restaurant rows. The locals insisted the revenue would go out of the County to the developers and investors anyway, that the old Pier, boardwalk and restaurants were doing fine and development would only cause overcrowding and traffic congestion.

The developers insisted that the current unemployment rate was seven percent and these improvements would create jobs. The locals didn't answer. They established a Planning Commission that banned high-rises. The Commission voted down the beachfront development package.

The Oceansport Inn remained loved as a source of commerce, reviled as a source of crowds, a shelter for tourists, an eyesore and the cause of an eclipsed beach. The Inn could not seem to shake the developer's vision.

Our Christmas party at the Oceansport Inn was infused with this melancholic legacy. Tammy kept threatening to leave. Le Blanc lay on his back under the Christmas tree, his head propped on a present. He swatted at tinsel with the tips of his fingers. Chester brought his girlfriend the sex therapist; she came swathed in a polyester jumpsuit of leopard skin design. She sulked. Hans and his wife sat by the Christmas tree holding hands. Alice continually remarked, "She's a pretty one," referring to the bulb of whipped cream on HTZ's Irish coffee, or the way a chestnut had popped open while roasting.

Once the bonuses had been passed out, the prospect of eating had been exhausted and we had settled down over a Christmas Eve beer, Chester turned his head toward the hallway, where screams had erupted.

Le Blanc jumped up in a jerk of reflex, rushing for the bar counter, then a corner seat, and finally coming back to his own place under the tree. Le Blanc's wife Maria hurled through the door.

"You!" she accused HTZ, threatening him with Le Blanc's foot-long level, which he used to balance pool tables. Maria approached HTZ and decimated his beer bottle with the metal bar. "Pervert," she called him. "Insidious viper."

Maria went around to each table, methodically scooping up each bonus check and subsequently, as if in return for the payment, smashing the respective beer bottle with the leveler.

Without intervention, Maria assaulted the Christmas tree itself, swatting at the glass ornaments, walloping the presents under the tree, breaking everything she had the strength to harm, but not disturbing Le Blanc, Hans, or his wife.

Our Christmas elf whooshed out of the room, white envelopes stuffed with bonus checks flapping in one hand, silver level in the other, the tube of liquid smashed now, the bubble escaped. She looked triumphant, like the beauty queens I had seen astride the Thunderbirds two months before, with their white gloves and silver staffs, that same crazed smile.

An Ordinary Man

On New Year's Eve I started at dawn and worked my route at breakneck speed to make time for myself. I wanted to witness both the surfing tournament and Le Blanc's testimony.

89

The waves at the Bluff are highest in winter. When I reached the north point of the cliffs that day, I was almost afraid. The waves were tremendous—larger than I'd ever seen them, waves I imagined could be found only on the north shore of Oahu. But since we had stolen the contest from the islands, I supposed we welcomed the equivalent conditions.

The boys standing by their surfboards on the cliffs appeared nonplussed by the dangerous conditions. But their casual swagger was in some way a key to their success. The boys needed that attitude of defiance, that arrogant confidence to balance and spin their boards in those waves.

A judging stand had been erected at the north end of the Bluff. The tournament sponsors had speakers and microphones installed so the contestants could hear when their heats began and ended. The boys wore vests over their wetsuits; the colors indicated which class they would surf in and the numbers identified them.

Sweetwater Police had anticipated the crowds and cordoned off the road that wended its way along the Bluff. I parked the truck at my apartment and walked up toward the judging stand. The spectators had taken up positions along the cliff, but they were too close to the edge. The tournament sponsors got on the loudspeaker and warned the crowds to move back, that large waves breaking could sweep them out to sea. But the crowd wouldn't budge, so the police stepped in and tried to move them back. The combination of crowds, police, and loudspeaker warnings, together with the ambulance that was parked near the judging stand in case of injuries, gave the scene the look and sound of a crime scene or a rock concert.

The masters had already competed, and of course Nick Tatum had won. The junior class had just finished competing. These were boys ages seven to thirteen. They were not really beginners, but they were the youngest group invited to compete on these waves. First place went to one of the boys I had seen talking to Nick Tatum a few months before—one of the boys with shark teeth imbedded in his board.

The advanced group was up next—young men ages fourteen to twenty-nine. Most of the contestants were in high school. I looked around for Kenny Sears. I found him in front of the judging stand, suited up and waxing his board. I had expected him to pick an old reliable board and wetsuit for the contest, equipment he knew was dependable, or believed lucky. But his royal blue Tatum wetsuit with silver stripes looked brand new, and so did the Tatum short board, silver with blue stripes and a blue fin. He was probably the only surfer competing who was not only seaworthy but color coordinated. Photographers clamored for pictures and Kenny obliged them. I took up my post by the payphone, but I couldn't see over the crowd, so I ventured out into that forbidden territory at the edge of the cliff, by the stairwell, and watched the advanced group cast out. Kenny saw me as he went down the stairs, reached out with his free hand, and pulled on a strand of my hair.

There were no surprises in the heat—Kenny caught the better waves, his turns and spins were more dazzling, his rides longer, his entries onto the waves smooth and his dismounts crisp. It was really no contest; I was sure he had won. I wanted to stay and watch Kenny receive his trophy and be photographed again with Nick Tatum, but it was after one, and I had to get to the courthouse for Le Blanc's testimony.

It was evident from the attorney's selection that he didn't want any of Sweetwater Music and Vending's clients on the jury. During jury selection both the Defense and Prosecution had routinely asked the prospective jurors where they worked, and if they ever used coffee, candy, soda, food or cigarette machines, or any pinball or video games, pool tables or jukeboxes when they socialized. Everyone who answered yes to these questions had been bumped from the jury. It was clear no one who even blindly played pinball in a corner bar without ever hearing of Sweetwater Music had been chosen.

It must be standard to eliminate any bias connected with the workplace, but after everyone was eliminated, the attorneys were left with five housewives, four junior college students including the alternate, and four fisher-men, all of whom were complaining of hardship.

I scrutinized the two attorneys, trying to gauge what they expected to yield from that day's testimony. The Defense looked like he hadn't slept all night. He looked like a jogger or a shortstop on one of the County softball teams. He seemed flexible, sympathetic, and uncertain of what the outcome of the trial might be. He was not an absolutist.

The Prosecution had the air of knowing exactly what would happen. He looked as if he occupied a fourteen-room Victorian home on the beach, with a huge bay window in his upstairs study. He sucked on his pipe in a tender way, as if he were thinking of a woman.

I saw Dante, B&B and Glenda look over at me as Le Blanc took the witness stand. They had been called as witnesses to support Le Blanc's testimony. They knew the dangers of testifying; Le Blanc had warned them.

Le Blanc did not look like himself sitting in the chair attached to the witness stand, leaning his shoulders in toward the podium so his soft voice could be heard through the microphone. He looked ordinary, like he could be anyone, some guy off the street. He did not look like the now-demoted supervisor of a pinball, jukebox and vending machine company who, under the direction of his boss HTZ, had engaged the whole town in clandestine and illegal gambling, drug dealing and prostitution activities, using the Sweetwater Music and Vending operation as a front, with HTZ orchestrating and financing the operation, with HTZ reaping an inordinate share of the profits. No, Le Blanc looked like an ordinary man, despite the fact that he was up on the witness stand describing these horrors to the jury.

The attorney for the Defense asked him the preplanned questions in quiet, sympathetic tones. The Prosecution was out of his mind with rage, interrupting every third sentence to issue an objection on the grounds that he could not see the relevance of this testimony. It was inexcusably time-consuming to the Court. The judge overruled the Prosecution each time, nodding to the Defense to continue. Once the judge did interrupt Le Blanc's testimony to remind the jury that Le Blanc, like all witnesses, was testifying under oath. If lying, Le Blanc would be guilty of perjury. If not lying, Le Blanc could be implicating himself and a large portion of townspeople in criminal activities for which they could be investigated, tried and jailed.

Le Blanc told the jury how cocaine and heroin were sold to the Jail inmates, and smuggled into the Jail inside the crotches of women's underwear. He described to the jury how nipple diameter bets were placed. The housewives on the jury went wild. The Prosecution's objections became more frenzied. Le Blanc told about the prostitution in various bars and other establishments, describing

B.F. Manta's ever-popular Cosmic Communion, which HTZ sponsored and from which he drew a percentage. He explained that the Beauty Pageant was bet upon and the outcome fixed; the same held true for the Annual Surfing Championships.

When the audience and jury were enthralled, Le Blanc suggested that Chester had been roped into an ugly illegal situation which was way beyond his scope, and which his boss insisted Chester engage in if he wanted to keep his job. Le Blanc began to cry, overcome by the perversity of the situation. It looked as if he were crying for Chester, who had been forced into these crimes by HTZ like an innocent forced into sex.

The Prosecution wanted to object again. He was utterly convinced that no iota of this testimony was going his way, but he could not object to a man crying on the witness stand without making himself look like a brute. So the Prosecution said nothing and gazed over at the jury box, trying to gauge how the fishermen were reacting.

Le Blanc finished by testifying that to his knowledge, HTZ had arranged trysts for Chester so that HTZ could play the role of voyeur, and Chester had no idea the girls were under eighteen.

In my hubris I thought Le Blanc might want my comfort after the testimony, but he was ensnared by reporters and surrounded by police, so I couldn't reach him. I finished my route and went home, hoping, by some gothic throwback in my character, that he'd be waiting for me there. All through my route and on the way home I kept chiding myself for not having figured it out—the drugs, the prostitution, the gambling; I should have known all along. How simple it all seemed to me now. I was disillusioned, but in an infantile way, like a child who had just been told there was no Santa Claus. I scolded myself for that too.

When I arrived home Le Blanc was not waiting, of course, but Kenny Sears was. For a moment the miasma of self-reproach cleared and I remembered his surfing. Here was a young boy who, despite his drugs and vanity, could do something well, something that was exciting and beautiful to watch. There was a pureness in this that comforted me. "Congratulations," I said. "You won, didn't you?"

He followed me up the walk without saying a word. When we were inside he handed me the afternoon edition of the *Sweetwater Carillon*. On the front page was a wet-down but enthusiastic Kenny Sears, one arm around Nick Tatum, the other cradling his trophy. The headline read: *SURFING TOURNAMENT RIGGED* and the photo caption said: *Are they really the best?* Next to the Tournament article was a piece on Le Blanc's testimony. That headline read: *THIEVES, SWINDLERS AND PERVERTS—ONE WITNESS' TESTIMONY.* A tiny photo of a beleaguered Le Blanc was imbedded in the text.

Figuring it was a mild offense compared to the ones we'd been hearing about, I offered Kenny a beer. "Is it true?" he said. "Is it really rigged?" I shrugged and told him I only knew what he did. He refused the beer. "But you know this guy," he insisted, pointing at Le Blanc's sorry photo. "I've seen you with this guy."

I told him he was the best—it was so obvious. What difference did it make if the judging was rigged. He would have won anyway. "Who says I'm the best?" he answered. "Who knows what the judges would have said if they weren't paid off. Who says?" I told him there wasn't a guy out there who came anywhere near surfing as well as he did. "Oh, what do you know," he said. "You're just in love with me." He picked up the newspaper and folded it with a great flourish, then buzzed out of the house as if all his synapses were firing at once.

I had bought my own afternoon edition of the *Sweetwater Carillon*, surreptitiously out of a machine. I was reading all the articles relating to the trial and Le Blanc's testimony, as if I hadn't been there myself, when Le Blanc finally showed up. He let himself in the kitchen door. He was rummaging around in there, and from the din of pots and pans he showed no signs of migrating into the main room, so I went to him. When he saw me he smiled, but it was a disjointed smile that made him look sheepish. "So now you know what the bank is," he said. I inspected the bag of groceries on the kitchen table, and removed the lids from the pots on the stove. I asked him if he thought I was a stupid jerk. "Just ingenuous," he said. Then he said that he was the jerk, that they all were for going along with it, and I should throw him out. I wanted to tell him I thought he was brave, but I knew him better now. I asked him what we were having for dinner. "*Poisson à la façon de grandmère,*" he said. I asked him what Poisoned Grandmother entailed. He told me it was a French fish stew his grandmother had taught him.

At 3am under the half moon the sea looks metallic. In a backdrop without sunlight, without industrial or traffic noises and with no human buffer, the sound of the waves is deafening. Life has been left to itself; the sea menaces.

As the sky lightens angles appear, telephone poles become visible, outlines of shops are discernible, people can be recognized getting into cars to go to early jobs at the cement plant. The more the light, the more is sapped from the sea's menace. It is a false menace, born of our imagination. The ocean is the same night and day, tides approaching and receding, waves smoother or rougher depending on the storms. It is simply our outlook that menaces.

But there is something undeniably eerie, this early in the morning, with the darkness to fuel our imaginations and the sun half up, there is something undeniably threatening about the sight of a bloated wetsuit, a topple of yellow curls protruding from the top, floating limp and mute into the soup of the waves, where finally it beaches, wetsuit, body and board, all inextricable.

The area had been cordoned off, and no one was allowed anywhere near the operations. Washed up on the beach was a surfer, sixteen, still clad in full wetsuit, his short board attached with the traditional leader strap. He was drowned.

The police chief delivered routine directions; the boy was packed off to the coroner's office where a thorough autopsy would be performed. By noon the news reports would reveal that Kenny Sears had drowned at midnight, most likely of a drug overdose. By evening, rumors would be widespread that he had committed suicide because he'd found out the surfing championships were rigged, and he'd even left a note, attached to the steering wheel of his car.

When I came back to the apartment the lights were on, and Le Blanc was sitting up in bed, smoking his pipe. I told him Kenny Sears had killed himself because of the Tournament being rigged. "Do you blame me?" he said. I told him Kenny had come by that afternoon, and I had said the wrong thing again. "Don't tell me you blame yourself," he said.

The Beauties

The six weeks of deliberations were over and the jury was in chambers to reach a final decision. I couldn't help but imagine what it would be like. The now seasoned members of the jury would be accustomed to their assigned seats in the jury box, not these chambers where they were sequestered without a mediator and forced to make up their minds. They would feel displaced, and frankly, frightened. The trial had proceeded for six weeks as predicted, with no unusual events except for Le Blanc's testimony during the second week of the trial. The jury had felt themselves merely spectators. Now they would have to put forth logic, analysis, and moral conviction. They would have to talk in a group. They would have to sentence a child molester to a long prison term, or release a weak man, manipulated by his boss into a series of dubious trysts with minors. None of them relished the responsibility.

It had taken the jury two full weeks of deliberation to reach a final verdict. When the jurors filed into the courtroom, looking as if they were the ones to be condemned, the presiding judge was already seated in his stuffed chair behind the podium. Both attorneys sat attentive and poised at their respective tables and a small inconspicuous group had gathered in the audience seats.

Amid the bland attire of long heavy coats, a tall blond woman seated next to Dante caught my eye. She was exquisite; her ashen hair held up in a voluptuous tumble, her face powdered a velvety white, her sultry blue eyes accented with mauve shadow. I wished it were not a biting March morning, and the woman would have taken off her coat. She must have been in her mid-fifties, and looked strikingly similar to the femme fatale movie actresses of the 1930s, Marlene Dietrich for example. I decided I must see her up close.

The Bailiff called the court to order. The judge asked for the verdict. The foreman rose from her seat composed, as if this were all routine. She delivered the verdict of guilty. The judge announced that he would deliver the penalty after review.

Hans tugged on his anchor but otherwise remained motionless, as if the verdict had been delivered on him. The Defense beat his fist solidly on the table but did not utter a word. The Prosecution would look no one in the eye and rushed to assemble his documents. It occurred to me that he might prosecute Le Blanc and Hans, B&B, and Davey the guard, and let HTZ go free.

"Going, Mr. Prosecutor?" a baritone voice admonished from the audience.

The Bailiff moved to get up, but the judge put his hand on his shoulder. The tall blond woman, my Marlene Dietrich look-alike, stood up. The Prosecution had turned around to answer the remark and now could not take his eyes off her.

The woman pushed her coat from her shoulders and let it drop onto the chair. She was dressed in a white shoulder fur, and underneath, a strapless yellow dress, clinging all the way down and slit up to mid-thigh. A pair of cream-colored pumps supported her. The woman was so much of a period piece that no one considered why she had worn such a costume into the courtroom. White elbow gloves covered her hands and forearms. The woman's legs were shaped to delight, like one of the Beauty Pageant winners from thirty years back. They did not make legs like that anymore. I wondered if perhaps this was one of the early Miss California winners, come back to make a statement.

Then I recognized him. It was Brent, the owner of the Blue Lagoon, dressed in drag. Brent had shaved from head to toe and donned a cocktail gown, as he was inclined to do most Halloweens. Instead of the rosewood cane to support his left leg, Dante was employed to brace him at the hip. He was seated next to Brent, his arm walled up under Brent's fallen coat. Le Blanc leaned in to whisper to me. "Miss California, 1949," he said. I looked over at him. He nodded. He wasn't kidding.

"Why don't you convict me?" the voluptuous blond admonished in her baritone.

That was enough for the Bailiff. He moved toward the outspoken blond, intending to usher her out of the room. The four policemen who up until now had stood inconspicuously in the four corners of the courtroom converged on its center, two surrounding Chester and his defense attorney, two approaching Brent.

Dante tossed Brent his rosewood cane so he could stand on his cream-colored pumps without assistance. Brent fled the courtroom, wailing at the Prosecution, "We missed you these past months Sammy, roped any new boys, or won't they have you?"

Realizing this was more an indictment than a riot, calculated to bring shame but not general disruption, and fearing media coverage, the Bailiff and police didn't stop Brent and Dante from leaving in a flourish, nor did they attempt to press charges. When the Bailiff and police had returned to the courtroom alone, Le Blanc took my hand and we slipped out to follow Brent.

We all arrived at the Blue Lagoon where Brent's fans were waiting. Hermes could not compete with Brent in approaching the sublime, but he did all right in his G-string and knee-high leather fringe borrowed from Larry. B&B came as himself in his straw boater. Brent entered on his cane and cream-colored pumps, which made him look even more like an aging movie actress. Waiting inside was the entire patronage of the Blue Lagoon and the B&B Card Room, the latter accompanied by their pet dogs. The retirees dropped the leashes and the dogs thrashed about, loving a crowd, yearning for affection. Glenda brought out her barmaids dressed in girdles and garters. The girls held tight to their cowboy friends who were equipped with red boots and spurs, leather vests and ranching hats. B.F. Manta came up behind them to welcome Brent. Even the UFO woman made an appearance. There she was in all her iridescent splendor, looking more like some exotic being who had risen from the sea than one dropped from the sky. B.F. assured Le Blanc the UFO woman would not be making any appointments or accepting any business. Le Blanc thanked him.

The punk rock and kung fu regulars of the Blue Lagoon had assembled a disco cassette with seven hours of continuous dance music. They swarmed around, blasting the Lagoon with the music's insistent beat. Brent was surrounded by a swarm of transvestites, prostitutes, well-wishers, retirees, dogs and disco queens, who had by now broken out the cases of champagne brought by Glenda. They were toasting over each other's heads.

Le Blanc had shaken his head to enough questioning faces that everyone knew Chester had been convicted. But Brent had done his share, and the mourners persisted. If this could not be a celebration, it would be a wake.

Brent was the first to step out on the dance floor, waving his cane in an alternate motion to counterbalance his hips. The kung fu and punk rock regulars joined in; they would have the most stamina as the afternoon waned. Even the old card players felt sufficiently uplifted to try, the younger dancers applauding them and the pet dogs biting their pant cuffs. The barmaids, cowboys, and UFO woman sat around the bar, pouring each other drinks, talking confidentially and watching the dancing. Dante kept an eye on things with B.F. Manta as they prowled from door to door, consulting between themselves. This was the first time I had seen Sweetwater's opposing factions at the same party and I wanted to watch, but Le Blanc took my arm and we got the hell out of there.

Household Gods

When Le Blanc arrived at the shop the next afternoon, Tammy and I were sitting in the warehouse, watching Hans get up our orders. We had been talking about HTZ, and whether or not he would be prosecuted for any of his illegal operations. Hans thought he was already being investigated. Tammy and Hans speculated about their future jobs once HTZ was incarcerated and Sweetwater Music and Vending folded. Tammy said she'd been offered a job at the Nuclear Missile Base, but she and Alice might stay at Sweetwater Music if it didn't fold and if it were bought by the right person. Hans said he might ask HTZ's financial backer to invest in a swimming club, which Hans would manage and lifeguard. I confessed I was going on my first archaeological dig in Greece that summer, and on to graduate school in Boston the following fall. I didn't tell them I had submitted my study of the socioeconomic correlates to cigarette brand preference as one of my research samples.

When Le Blanc came in we asked him what he would do. He said he had been looking around, and had offers from a beer distributor and a soft drink vendor. Hans said he was counting on all of us for his swimming club. Tammy asked him if he was putting us on. "Would I kid you?" he said, and then resumed his pleas for Le Blanc and the rest of us to come to work for him. Le Blanc told him to get the financing and then they would talk.

That's when HTZ came into the warehouse and said to Le Blanc, "So you still haven't found another job? Do you know why I haven't fired you since you testified?" Le Blanc said he imagined he wanted to show his best face to prevent being indicted himself. "That's right," HTZ said. "So why haven't you quit?" Le Blanc said he was working on it. HTZ leaned against the door to the warehouse. Tammy lit a cigarette. Hans continued to get the orders up and pretended not to be listening. I sat on a case of Snickers bars, paralyzed with fear.

HTZ wasn't finished. He said, "Your wife called me today. She was upset with me about all the illegal things I've made you do. I guess you never told her. How kind of you to shelter her from harm." Le Blanc said she'd known about it since Christmas Eve, when he'd warned her what he was going to testify. "I remember the little scene she made at the party. I guess the guilty verdict set her off again. It's brought out the confessional urge in her. When you get home she plans to tell you that I'm the one she's been having the affair with all these years, that little Scott is mine."

Tammy lunged at HTZ and tried to put out her cigarette in his eyes, but Hans restrained her. Le Blanc said he already knew. HTZ said, "I had been trying to convince her to take Scott and move in with me, but she wouldn't until now, she felt sorry for you. She didn't want you to be alone." We all looked at HTZ, as if we didn't believe what he was about to say. But he went ahead and said it. "So I told her you've been having an affair with Maya here, and that seemed to convince her."

Hans took up a position between Le Blanc and HTZ, expecting Le Blanc to lunge at him this time, but he didn't. He didn't do anything. He just said, *I already knew that*, and walked out, without looking at anyone.

After Le Blanc left that afternoon, no one could find him. HTZ said that maybe he'd gone on a drunk, or left town, or was aimlessly swinging his legs over the pier. Tammy called his house; Maria said his pipes were missing from their holder next to his TV chair in the den. Hans noticed that his toolbox was missing from the shop.

I went home for a while; I was hoping Le Blanc would show up there, but after a few hours I realized he wouldn't. Then I went out looking. I checked the diners, bars, pool halls and bowling alleys we used; then I drove by the establishments on his route, and on that evening's repair list. I even checked MacKenzie's Pub in Emeryville. Then I checked the stops on my own list, the ones that would still be open.

At midnight I finally found him, in the sanctuary of the back room at B&B's, his pipes spread out on a poker table, the way another person might spread out his love letters or family photographs. Le Blanc had also brought with him pipe cleaners, sanders, polishers, three varieties of wood oils and a selection of rags and brushes from his toolbox. He had arranged the pipes in chronological order from left to right on the poker table: his clay pipe from high school, the corn cob pipe used during the burglar alarm business days, the brass pipe from his single father days, the mahogany pipe he smoked when he was courting Maria, his rosewood pipe—a wedding present from Maria.

Le Blanc had turned on the floodlights over the poker table. He worked through the night, brushing, polishing, oiling, and thinking of nothing. I sat there with him, but I knew there was nothing I could do or say to help him. He already knew that Maria wouldn't leave him, but eventually, she would cheat on him again. He knew that I had to go away, and even if I didn't, he would want me to. So he sat there, brushing, polishing, and oiling, exorcising the cuckold demons, the shame and remorse demons, the pride demons, and all the household gods living in him. He was still there in the morning when the reporters converged on his house and found him gone. He was still there when the D.A.'s office converged on the Sweetwater Hotel Dining Room for a stunned lunch. Le Blanc was in B&B's back room, polishing, and oiling, until dinnertime. When he packed up his toolbox, Le Blanc was a free man again.

"When are you leaving?" he asked me. I told him June. "That gives us some time," he said. I asked him what he meant. He said April and May. Then he asked me where I wanted to go for dinner.

Most Likely to Succeed

The residents gathered from all sections of Sweetwater County to witness the restoration. Brent himself was scheduled to return his own Miss California 1949 photograph to its rightful place on the Sweetwater Hotel Dining Room wall, between Miss California 1948 and 1950. The picture had been taken down the day before for this occasion and in the space where Brent's photo would be reinstalled a square of brightly colored wallpaper now shone.

The local media had made a celebrity of Brent in the three days following his brilliant courtroom performance. Local reporters rummaged through news clippings and documents of the 1940s and 1950s pageants, revealing all the minutiae of this dubious winner. According to that day's *Sweetwater Carillon*, Brent had entered the contest as Brenda, keeping the other facts of his high school career intact: President of the Drama Club, Vice President of the Speech Club, acting member of the Debate Club, member of the school choir, performed in such high school musicals as *The Wizard of Oz*, *Forty Second Street* and *Top Hat*. Upon graduation he was voted Most Likely To Succeed.

In order to provide three childhood snapshots required to enter the contest, Brenda had borrowed from his sister. But for more recent pictures Brenda had taken his own, photographed with great care one weekend while his parents had gone to Lodi.

Santa Del Mar, the obscure coastal town of five hundred residents where Brenda was born, would not follow the Pageant on their radios. If they had they could not have recognized their hometown drama club hero. Brent had allegedly set off to Oregon to work as a lumberjack throughout the spring and summer. In fall he would start college at Oregon State. When he did start three months late, he brought along his scepter and crown, like a king dispossessed of his country. He had left home for good.

What he found in Sweetwater were a sense of self and a place to come back to. In Sweetwater he reigned. After college he went south to Hollywood, working as a stagehand at MGM and eventually as a set manager, until he had saved enough money to open the Blue Lagoon.

The crowd cheered Brent now as he stepped up to the wall of Beauties, where only one bright patch of wallpaper was visible. He had returned to wearing his three-piece suit and Panama hat. His rosewood cane supported him. His beard and eyebrows had not had time to grow back; without them Brent looked more vulnerable, though still magnetic. He bowed graciously to the adoring crowd and tipped his hat, but would provide them with none of the drama of his court appearance. He would not even speak. He returned the picture to the wall, admiring for a moment the youthful beauty captured inside the frame. He opened the glass case where the official crown and scepter sat and gave them each a loyal kiss. Finally he had come into his own.

The women in the crowd burst into shameless weeping; only they seemed to feel the cruelty of chance. The photographers from the *Sweetwater Carillon*, eager for pathos, rushed to snap pictures of these women, their noses half hidden by their handkerchiefs.

EPILOGUE
HANS' SWIM CLUB

The Defense is preparing for Chester's appeal. The Defense is confident and Chester believes in him. B&B closed down his bank. The lifers still play cards in there with a frenzy, and they still bet, but usually just for a beer, or a sandwich, or a pack of Pall Malls.

That is the way it looks all over the County now. The barmaids at MacKenzie's refuse to take anyone into the bathroom. No packages of underwear can be found at the jail and no tape measure can be seen flying across the tops of pool tables or bar counters. No one bets at the surfing championships or beauty pageant. B.F. Manta won't introduce anyone to the Cosmic Communion. Dante keeps cocaine out of the Blue Lagoon.

We used to be lighthearted. We tolerated each other's quirks, foibles, and idiosyncrasies of gender. Chester sunbathed nude. I lusted privately after young surfers. B.F. dreamed of the Cosmic Communion happening to him. Alice saw the world as entirely female. Dante mourned the Duke. Brent wanted his true beauty and achievements revealed. Glenda wanted to be loved. In those days it was eccentric, fun. But we became lazy and scared and HTZ got greedy, and that's how we got sucked in. Now we're left with a series of mistakes and misunderstandings that have escalated into a series of indictments. We have to try to regain the town we had, and fight to keep it from becoming a parody of the original.

Our saving grace is Hans. He will restore our peace of mind soon. Last month he opened a place in Sweetport called Hans' Swim Club. It is a restaurant with a pool in back. He lets everyone swim naked, but that's all—no gambling, no prostitution, no fooling around. He gives the massages himself and opens up the sauna now and then. Hans hired all of us who are not in jail—Alice, Tammy, Le Blanc; I will be working with them on summer breaks during graduate school, and he's promised Chester a job when he gets out. Business was slow the first week, but now people are flocking to the Swim Club as if it's their only solace. It's the only thing people do in Sweetwater, besides listening to the grisly reports of HTZ's trial.

Anyway, Hans' Swim Club is the best place to be right now. It is going to be a hit. Hans might even become a cult figure. In the meantime, the rest of Sweetwater thinks Brent is their hero. Le Blanc will always be mine.

IN ONE ENORMOUS BED
LIKE CHILDREN

After he made love to his wife, Pearse lay on his back and waited until he could hear her steady breathing. When he was sure she was asleep he checked the time. The illuminated numbers on the digital clock glowed in the dark bedroom. It was midnight. He slipped out of bed and carefully put on his clothes, trying not to wake her. As he was leaving the room she said, "Where are you going, dear?"

"Out for cigarettes," he said. "Go back to sleep."

"You don't need to smoke now," she said. "Come back to bed."

"I'll only be a minute," he said. "Sleep."

Pearse left his apartment on the Upper West Side and took a taxi across town to see his mistress. Since they worked together he usually saw her at lunch. But the next morning Centrex Corporation was sending him on a two-week Manager's Retreat at the Banstock mansion in the Adirondacks. He had never been away from his mistress for more than a weekend, and he wanted to see her before he left. This was Pearse's first affair. He had never mixed work with romance before. The combination made his life more exciting than it had ever been with his wife, so much so that Pearse thought he might be in love with his mistress—really in love. He wanted to know.

When Pearse returned home at four in the morning his wife was sitting up in bed reading. He had forgotten the cigarettes. "Damn," he said.

"Who is she?" she said. She took a Kleenex from the carton on her lap and blew her nose.

Pearse knelt down on the floor next to the bed. "Have you been crying all this time?" he said. "I never would have dreamed—"

"She must not be going on the retreat if you felt compelled to go over there now," she said.

Pearse had no idea what to say. He had never seen his wife look so lost. When the boys were born, and she became withdrawn and listless, he had felt some resentment smoldering in her. But now it seemed she had no recourse. It was as if someone close to her had died. He took her hand; it was ice cold. "Darling," he said.

The managers at the retreat were all from different companies; none of them knew each other. It was an intense two weeks however, and they got to know each other almost instantly. It was as if they had to fit in as much confession and intrigue as they could, before they returned to their families.

Pearse was friendly but tried to remain aloof. He was still shaken by his wife's grief and didn't want to complicate his guilt with another betrayal. Everyone else was sleeping together though, and he felt left out. He found a woman named Vanessa attractive, so he was relieved when an older man named Jason pursued her.

One evening in the middle of the first week, Pearse went out drinking with Vanessa, Daniel and Rana, at a bar in the little resort town closest to the Banstock mansion. Evelyn and Edward didn't come; they were spending all their time alone. Daniel and Rana had obviously been sleeping together, which left Pearse with Vanessa. As much as he liked her, Pearse felt uncomfortable being paired with her. He thought she would bring Jason, but the older man didn't come.

Daniel and Rana sat on one side of the table, Pearse and Vanessa on the other. Vanessa was shivering in her thin blouse, so Pearse offered her his tweed jacket. She put it on. Now it will smell like her and haunt me, he thought. But she began to talk about Jason.

"I need your advice," she told the three of them. "Jason is really pressuring me to have an affair. I don't know what to do."

"Whatever you do," Pearse said, "don't tell your husband. And don't get caught." He didn't want to pretend he had morals, but he didn't want to encourage her. He figured this response was the best compromise.

The cocktail waitress came and they ordered the specialty of the house: Bloody Marys in quart canning jars garnished with a celery stalk. "I'd have to tell my husband," Vanessa said. "Our only rule is total honesty."

Pearse winced. She was so young. "Then why do it at all?" Daniel said. "If that's your policy it must be a healthy marriage." Daniel was bored with his wife so he had slept with Rana. What was one more betrayal? Now he was disgusted with himself.

"Jason's been around," Vanessa said. "I could learn from him. But he won't get close to me unless we go to bed. He says I'm a tease. I want the emotional intimacy but I don't want to hurt my husband."

Pearse watched Vanessa chew the leaves off her celery stalk and search their faces for a response. She was so ingenuous. "Jason's a desperate character," Daniel said. "His third marriage is on the rocks. If you do it, make sure he understands you're not serious. It's your responsibility not to hurt him."

"Listen to all of you," Rana said. She put her drink down and shifted impatiently in her chair. "Hurting your husband, hurting Jason. What about your hurt? I say do what *you* want to do."

"Jason won't do what I want," Vanessa said.

"Whatever you do, don't tell your husband," Pearse repeated. He twirled his celery stalk in his drink, rattling the ice.

"You just got caught, didn't you," Rana said smartly.

Pearse nodded. "Well what's your arrangement?" he said. He knew she slept with everyone. He couldn't be the only one whose marriage was a wreck.

"We do what we want," Rana said.

"And you're happy?" Vanessa said, amazed.

"No," Rana said. She pulled the celery stalk out of her drink and sucked out the alcohol.

"What do you do?" Pearse asked Daniel. He felt absurd, like he was taking a survey. But now that they were all talking about it, he figured, *What the hell.*

"My wife and I keep each other honest," Daniel said. He added, "When we get bored we fool around." He winked.

"And does that work?" Vanessa asked.

"Not really," Daniel admitted.

"If only we didn't want more than we have," Vanessa said, hugging herself in Pearse's jacket.

"What a mess," Pearse said. He hadn't suspected things were this bad.

Pearse sat down in the phone booth in the lobby of the Banstock mansion. The booth lit up when he wedged the door shut. He preferred to talk to his wife in the dark, but the booth would not be soundproof with the door ajar. He settled for a bright privacy. Life was a series of disappointing compromises, he thought as he dialed his own number. There was no possibility for innocence, no pure feeling.

Pearse's oldest son Alex answered the phone. He was a grown-up five. "Daddy," he said, "did you go away because I ran into your study Tuesday night when you were trying to work?"

"No," Pearse said. "It's a business trip. It has nothing to do with you."

"Don't lie," Alex said. "You can tell me."

"Alex, don't make things up," Pearse said gently. "I'll tell you when something's wrong. Has your mother been nice?"

"Nicer than usual," Alex said. "I think she feels bad 'cause you're mad at me."

"I told you I'm not mad," Pearse said. "Would you call your mother to the phone?" Pearse could hear Alex telling her, *Daddy's not mad at me for running into the study.* It was a rule: Don't bother your dad when he's working.

"Hello?" his wife said. Her voice was so stiff it made Pearse feel like an insurance salesman.

"I'm going to tell you the truth," he said gravely.

"I'm listening," she said.

"I'm not going to see her anymore," he said. "It's over." Sure, he and his mistress had work in common. This excited him, and he'd never been excited by his wife. But he had been through hell with his wife. He couldn't hurt her. He didn't want to lose her.

"Have you told her yet?" his wife said.

"She's not here," he said. "Don't you think I should tell her in person?"

"I don't know," his wife said.

"I'll call her right now then," Pearse said. "Whatever you want." He sensed he had lost his advantage.

"I don't mean that," she said. "I've been having a good time here alone, since you've been gone. I'm surprised. I like being independent. I like the children."

"So what do you mean?" Pearse said. "You don't want me to break it off with her?"

"You damn well better break it off with her," she said. "Or I'm not letting you back into this apartment."

"Then what do you mean, 'I don't know,' " he said.

"I mean I might divorce you anyway," she said.

On the last night of the retreat they had a party. In the living room Vanessa sat in the large upholstered chair and Evelyn sat beside her, half on the arm of the chair, half in Vanessa's lap. They had their arms around each other. Edward sat opposite them on the velvet couch, smoking his pipe and watching. The others were in the back of the room.

"Have you ever slept with a woman?" Evelyn asked Vanessa.

"Why no," Vanessa said, astonished. "Have you?"

"No," Evelyn said. "But after all this," she waved her hand around the room at the others, "we might try it," she said, brushing the hair out of Vanessa's eyes.

"It's an idea," Vanessa conceded.

Edward nodded his approval. "I could put you up in a loft in the Financial District where you wouldn't be bothered," he said.

"Would you come visit?" Vanessa said.

"Of course," Edward and Evelyn said in unison. They all buckled over laughing.

In the back of the room, Jason was holding forth on de Kooning. He had an oversized art book cracked open across his legs; Pearse and Daniel sat beside him on the floor. Jason leaned his back up against the swooning couch where Rana was lying down, and she swung her arm over his shoulder. While he talked she stroked his collar and ear with one of her long fingernails. Daniel passed a joint among them. When Jason had his lungs full of smoke, he got up on his knees, bent over Rana, and blew the smoke into her mouth. Pearse and Daniel watched them kiss, Jason's Adam's apple bobbing up and down, his hands passing lightly over Rana's breast. He pulled her down onto the floor to join the group.

Pearse was talking to Daniel about his marriage again. He was telling him how his wife changed after she had the boys. "She got so depressed," Pearse said.

"Oh, but that's normal," Daniel said.

"No, not this," Pearse said. "She wasn't interested in sex, she wasn't interested in anything."

"Did she breast-feed?" Rana asked.

"Yes," Pearse said.

"That was her mistake," Rana said. "I would never share my breasts with the children. They belong to my husband." Pearse and Daniel exchanged looks.

"How about doing it in new surroundings," Daniel suggested. Pearse had talked to him at length about his marriage troubles, so Daniel knew the problem was current. "How about the Brooklyn Bridge?"

"Tell the truth Daniel," Rana said. "Where have you done it that's so unusual?"

"On the roof, in a broom closet, underneath a flight of stairs, and in the elevator," Daniel said succinctly.

"I grew up in Oklahoma," Pearse said. "We never did anything like that."

Daniel said, "It's Rana's turn."

"Too complicated," Rana said, and looked around for her drink. She tried to get up but Jason held her arm.

"Tell us," he said.

"I was sitting by a stream. Our cow had just given birth, and this boy who worked for my father threw the placenta against the fence. "

Daniel began to howl. "Daniel," Pearse scolded. He thought this might be the pure feeling he was looking for.

"Can't you see she's putting you on Pearse," Daniel said.

"That's bad for the cow," Jason said. "You're supposed to let the cow eat the placenta after she gives birth. She needs to recoup the iron and vitamins."

Daniel doubled over on the carpet and tried to get his breath. "So let her finish," Pearse said. "She didn't finish." They waited for Rana to continue.

"Oh, that's all," she said. "He threw the placenta against the fence and we made love. That's all."

"That's all?" Pearse said.

"I feel sick," Daniel said, and joined Edward on the velvet couch in the front of the room.

Jason helped Rana up and led her over to the fireplace, where they lay down together. She was cold, so she took Jason's suit jacket off the back of Vanessa's chair to put on. Vanessa and Evelyn shifted forward together so Rana could pull the jacket loose.

"I think the girls have a thing going," Rana whispered to Jason, but he had his hands covering his face and his chest was heaving. "What is it?" Rana said. She tried to pry his hands loose, but he was too strong for her. "What?"

She wiped the tears off his temples with the back of her hand.

"My wife hasn't slept with me in three years."

"Now, now," Rana said. "It's the last night." Then she said, "What about where you've done it. You didn't say."

"I don't want to," he said. "It cheapens it."

Edward repacked his pipe and watched Daniel watch Jason. "What happened over there?" Edward said. "Was there a fight?"

"Oh no, nothing like that," Daniel said. "Just some boasting. Why?"

"Because Jason's crying and Pearse is over there sulking in his drink."

Daniel turned to locate Pearse. Left alone, he had climbed up onto the swooning couch, and sat there looking down into the bottom of his gin glass. "It's the last night," Daniel said. "Tomorrow we face our wives, husbands and children."

"The children, that's different," Edward said.

Daniel looked at Evelyn and Vanessa. "So what have you three been talking about?" He remembered Vanessa's policy of total honesty and wondered how she would explain Evelyn to her husband.

"Arrangements," Edward said, lighting his pipe.

Rana stood up and wrapped the sides of Jason's suit jacket around her. "Don't go," Jason said to her. "Dance with me."

"Dance with me hell," she said. "Look at you." She turned to the others and said, "We can see each other again if we want to. Why is this like a farewell?"

Daniel shrugged. "Look at Pearse," he said, nodding his head toward the man sitting on the swooning couch, his gin glass held with both hands between his legs, his head thrown back in an attitude of anguish.

"Pearse!" Rana said. She marched over to him, sat down on the floor between his legs, took his drink out of his hands and set it down out of reach. She tapped on his knee with her long fingernails. "Darling," she said.

Pearse lifted his head off the wall and looked down at her. "I think we should all sleep together tonight," he said. "In one enormous bed like children."

"Come join the group Pearse," Rana said. She stood up and held out her hand to him.

"I can't," he said. "I can't bear it."

Daniel turned the music on and danced around Vanessa and Evelyn. Edward watched, taking long draws on his pipe. Jason stood up and monopolized Vanessa, holding her tight against him and kissing her. Daniel and Evelyn danced together.

Pearse let Rana lead him over to the fireplace. They lay down there together. "I think we should all sleep here together tonight," Pearse said to the dancers. "After all, it's the last night."

They nodded their heads. When each of them became too tired or too despondent, they lay down by the fireplace with Pearse and Rana. By the time the music stopped they were all asleep there, heads nestled in stomachs, legs thrown over hips, arms around waists, faces cradled in shoulders.

Pearse woke up at dawn. He looked around him. Some time during the night Edward had climbed on the velvet couch and curled up there away from the others. The traitor, Pearse thought. Daniel slept apart from Vanessa and Evelyn, who were so entangled Pearse could not make out whose limbs were whose. Jason and Rana were gone.

"I knew it," Pearse said. He had to go home that day and face his wife. Pearse went to Jason's room, opened the door without knocking, took off his clothes and got in bed next to Rana.

"Who is it?" Rana said, half asleep. "Who's there?"

"It's Pearse," Jason said, rolling over and embracing them both with his all-encompassing arm.

Rana put her hands on Pearse's waist and pulled him toward her. "I can't," he said.

"Let's," she said. "Jason won't mind."

"I can't betray my wife anymore," he said. "Can't we just lie here like children?"

By eight that morning they had all gone to their respective rooms to shower, dress, pack and think about their homecomings. By nine they were all seated at the breakfast table. Rana said, "I have to make an announcement." They all stopped eating and listened. "That boy I told you about, the one by the stream?" Rana said. She put down her fork. They nodded eagerly. "Well, he did throw the placenta against the fence, but I didn't make love with him."

Daniel started laughing. Vanessa and Evelyn looked at each other with puzzled expressions. Jason shook his head.

"You didn't make love with him?" Pearse said, incredulous. He couldn't stand it.

"I'm sorry," Rana said. "I had to tell you."

"You lied to us," Pearse said. "You made it sound so touching."

"I said I was sorry," Rana said.

The rest of them went back to their breakfasts. Pearse threw his linen napkin on the table, kicked his chair out from underneath him and stormed out of the room.

"Pearse, please," Rana said.

"I hate compromise," Pearse said as he shut the door behind him.

"What's bugging him?" Jason said. "He had as good a time as any of us." He shot a glance at Rana.

"It's the last day," Daniel explained. He went out to look for Pearse.

Daniel found Pearse leaning against his car, kicking the dirt with his boot. "Come back inside and eat your breakfast," Daniel said.

"I can't," Pearse said. "I'm wretched." He pulled at his hair.

"Your wife won't leave you," Daniel said.

"How do you know?" Pearse said.

"I know," Daniel said. "Come inside."

Pearse looked up at the dining room window. They were all huddled there, watching. "We're all wretched and disgusting," Pearse said.

"Rana was trying to be straight with you," Daniel said. "Trying it out before she goes home, maybe for the first time. It meant a lot to her."

Pearse laced his arms across his chest. He shook his head. Now he knew how his son Alex felt when the boy resisted.

"You'll do it again," Daniel said.

"Never," Pearse said, drawing back in horror. "I'll never cheat on her again."

Daniel held out his hand to Pearse. "For the last time," he said. "Come eat with us."

But Pearse refused. As he watched Daniel walk back to the dining room Pearse thought, *If my wife does leave me, I hope she doesn't take the children.* Then he wondered how he could possibly go on when the boys had grown up and moved away. He didn't know what he would do.

SAYINGS IN A GREEK LANDSCAPE

1. When You Drink the Water, Think of the Man Who Dug the Well

While Yergos was dressing for school he noticed that two fresh eggs were sitting on the ground below his windowsill. Was this a gift or charity? Had someone discarded the eggs? Was someone playing a trick on him?

Since he was an orphan living alone in an abandoned Monastery, Yergos even considered that God himself might have left the eggs. But Yergos, a boy of ten, didn't believe in God. His Greek Orthodox god had allowed his family to be forced from their home and farmland on the island of Imvros. They fled to Constantinople where the Muslim god lived by the sword. Yergos preferred the ancient Greek gods—quirky, vulnerable, impertinent.

Yergos was hungry. There was nothing else to eat this morning or any morning and he had to leave for school soon. Hunger squelched his wonderment and he ate the eggs.

But the eggs kept appearing. Every morning two eggs hugged the corner wall below Yergos' windowsill. There were plenty of other windowsills, he thought, on every wall of the Monastery, every wall in Constantinople. Yergos raced around the Monastery to find his was the only wall adorned. He fancied himself gifted, blessed, singled out. The eggs didn't even make him sick. All the same, Yergos kept alert now. He scrutinized anyone who lurked near the Monastery. He noticed any faces staring at him; he looked for faces full of longing, expressions that would reveal a stranger had designs on him. He waited for those who teased him to suddenly leave off and grow content. But none of this occurred.

So Yergos did what he thought he must do. When night came at the end of the second week of eggs, Yergos wrapped a blanket around himself and huddled outside his room, keeping the wall under the windowsill in full view. He would wait outside and see the benefactor for himself.

In the early morning when he could barely see, Yergos watched as the first egg was rolled carefully to the wall. There was a hole in the wall just under the windowsill and the squirrel inched slowly toward it, cradling the new egg in his arms. Just below the storage place the squirrel lost his grip, and easing back down the wall, left the egg below the windowsill. Yergos watched the squirrel leave and return with the second egg. He followed it back to the chicken coop. There was no benefactor, tormentor or trickster.

For several mornings afterward Yergos continued to eat the eggs brought by the squirrel, but they no longer held their taste and they left Yergos hungry. He did what he must. Just after dawn each morning he stole back to the chicken coop, returning the eggs the squirrel had brought. This satisfied Yergos, but he could not stay awake in the schoolroom or keep up with his studies. The schoolmaster kept him until the late afternoons. Winter was coming and the days shortened. Yergos never got home before dark. Finally one morning at the coop when Yergos had the eggs in his hands, the woman who owned the chickens confronted him.

"Thief!" the woman cried.

Yergos knelt down, returned the eggs to the straw without breaking them, stood up again and wiped his hands. "Yes," he said, feeling too guilty to explain about the squirrel. He started for school.

When the squirrel brought the eggs the next morning Yergos was waiting for it. He screamed and chased it with a stick, making sure it would be too frightened to come back. He patched the hole in the wall. A week passed and the eggs began to appear again.

Yergos wrapped his bed blanket around him and prepared to stay up all night, resolved that he must kill the squirrel. But in the morning it was the woman who came. She left the eggs, pausing to rub the fog off the window and glance inside at the empty bed. Yergos could not imagine why.

2. Eat Bubula Eat, What Future?

The waiter's stomach precedes him into the dining room. The waiter himself, Mr. Panagiotis, balances his tray on an extra fleshy stub protruding from the side of his smallest finger. He serves the dinner of ox tail soup, prodding and poking the girls with his stub. "I have in mind all persons who are natural objects of my bounty," he chirps and with a flourish Panagiotis designates the immediate women as these objects. Thus spent, Mr. Panagiotis grins with such intense satisfaction that he pushes air through his teeth. He tucks the empty tray under his arm and approaches three young university students who are slamming their backgammon chips fitfully around the board.

"Eat my sons eat! What future?" Mr. Panagiotis asks, looming over one of his charges, using his stub to stroke the inklings of the boy's afternoon growth of beard. They gaze up at his stub. They go back to their game. They needn't speak to Mr. Panagiotis. "Eat my sons, eat, you pay tomorrow!" he sings. He knows they never pay. He absorbs their accounts. They have worked out a system. Mr. Panagiotis winks at the boy who is being beaten at the game, while prickling the girl in the seat behind with his appendage, until she thinks she is being ravaged by a mosquito.

At the cashier's counter two waiters are fighting for possession of a meal. Usually the cashier sells the dish at the standard price to the waiter who ordered it, but not tonight. They are watching a soccer game on television and victory is imminent. "To the highest bidder then!" she cries. In the ensuing scuffle Panagiotis rescues the plate from behind the counter with the help of his deft stub. He serves it, free of charge, to the sullen boy who has lost double at backgammon. Greece wins the soccer game.

Mr. Panagiotis tucks the tray under his arm and patiently watches the boy eat. When he is finished Mr. Panagiotis bows deeply, removes the plate and says there is more ox tail soup for the others. On the way to the kitchen he fondles the cashier with his protrusion. She laughs. She absorbs his accounts. She is an object of his bounty.

A shipping merchant and his wife are vacationing. They want to eat. "Eat Bubula, eat! What future?" Mr. Panagiotis cries, rubbing his extra part against the wife's bare back. He will serve them his best feast.

It starts with lots of sweet wine to whet the appetite, and chunks of hot fresh bread dipped in a yogurt-garlic-dill cream. When they cannot wait any longer, so tempted by the wine, so aroused by the bread dipped in dill sauce, Mr. Panagiotis serves a tomato bulging with fresh shrimp, the shrimp drenched in olives and onion and blended with lemon. At the table Panagiotis adds a dash of salt, grinning with intense satisfaction and brushing against the merchant's wife as he leaves, to enhance her pleasure.

When they are not quite finished with the shrimp, Panagiotis brings the lamb, stuffed with marinated vegetables, seasoned with dill, garlic and oregano, roasted and barbecued in wine and wrapped tightly in grape vines. Panagiotis stands calmly next to the table while the couple ravages the lamb. When they are about to satisfy themselves the lamb is finished. Growling faintly somewhere deep in his throat, Panagiotis takes the plates away. When the wife's yearning has mounted almost to the point of despair, he brings the couple dessert.

He serves them Galataboureko, a sweet milky pastry filled with custard. Panagiotis watches as he allows the couple to finally satisfy themselves. He rests his protrusion on the woman's back, so that when she gets up to leave the stub strokes a path down her spine, causing her to shiver. She thanks him for the exquisite meal and the merchant pays him generously. "I have in mind, expressly, all persons who are natural objects of my bounty," Panagiotis declares, pocketing the money.

3. Oh My Black Donkey, Live till May and You Will Eat Green Green Grass

When the three of them, all Greeks, arrive at the only whitewashed building in this quarter of Constantinople, they feel like the Shades or the Trinity. They pass through the marble columns and enter a large room with a dome suspended over steaming windows. They take off their shoes and hand them to a waiting attendant. He gives each of them a number.

Barefoot, they race up the tiers, jostle among the couches. Each man grabs his own couch and tears off his clothes, folding them into the seat corner, never worrying about thefts or glances.

As Yergos is folding his last leaf of clothing another attendant comes. He has a stack of twelve towels piled high on one hand. The largest is for the pre-dry, another is to be tied around the waist, another is for the shoulders, with one he wraps his head in a turban, with the smallest he dries his hands and feet.

Blasted by the heat, Yergos goes directly to the square marble slab in the center of the steam room. The other two men run from fountain to pool, pool to pool, jumping into the hot and cold water in such succession that it blends into a sweet sting. Raging at each other, dipping into the opposite pool with ladles ready, they pour the icy and scorching water on their own heads, on each other.

Yergos watches them idly until the attendant comes with his woolly sheepskin and a hot bucket of soap. Yergos passes five coins to him and he rubs the skin against Yergos' skin, his kneecaps displacing themselves on the marble slab. When the attendant is finished Yergos rolls off into the adjacent pool.

Yergos goes to his bath. There are some completely private, but these three do not need one. Most are little compartments, and like a taverna you bring your backgammon board and stay as long as you like.

An attendant comes and, using Yergos' towel, dries him from the waist up. He waits while Yergos orders a drink. Staring up at the ceiling Yergos recalls one of the quince trees on his father's garden plot on the island of Imvros, with one of the settlers, as they called the Turks then, crouched on the first branch, breaking off twigs lined with fruit and dropping the twigs to the ground instead of picking quince by quince.

Yergos' father spotted him too and ordered him down. Thinking he was caught for stealing and had to assert his superior status, he pulled a knife. Yergos' father, nonplussed by heroics, hooked his walking cane around the settler and toppled him onto the twigs. The knife fell; the father picked it up, stabbed the quince tree and broke the knife blade off into the trunk, throwing the butt end away.

Still hooked by the cane, the settler watched Yergos' father as he demonstrated how to pick quinces properly.

The settler laughed and they went off together, arm in arm, Yergos' father leading him to a fine little pool where they pulled up watercress for lunch. Yergos' father drew a flask of olive oil from his pouch, insisting that the greens must be drenched in oil. They ate together.

At midnight the three men renounce the bath, dry and dress warmly because outside it snows. As they leave two Turks are positioned on the marble bathing slab, flexing their muscles and wrestling. They have drawn a crowd. Outside, Yergos' two companions disappear into the whitewashing snow.

Yergos seeks out the tiny Greek store around the corner. He buys a beer, a carton of olives, and a sandwich made of ultra thin slices of camel meat, preserved in oil and vinegar and stacked with three inches of the hottest red pepper between the slices. It makes him so thirsty he shall drink beer all night. Tomorrow Yergos leaves Constantinople for good.

4. Even the Multicolored Goat Would Laugh

Tasso was an Environmental Engineer. He dealt with hazardous waste, chemical dumplings, PCBs, vast networks of corroding bins languishing on expansive hidden lots near auto wrecking yards in New Jersey. But his specialty was garbage. He was doing his doctoral dissertation on the toxic waste produced by the average garbage dump. Since he couldn't test an entire dump he built a model: five cubic inches of dog food. It would produce methane gas and a doctoral degree.

"Garbage is my new topic," he shrugged, lighting a Kent. "That's what Environmental Engineering is about, trying to decide what to do with all the garbage, you see this?" He gestured up from his ears as if wisdom, like heat, rises. "These Americans here," he said, tamping his finger down on the tablecloth, "they like to drown theirs. The French vacuum it into tubes. The Greeks bury theirs. The Turks pile it up." He shook his head. "But the professors in the Engineering Department act like they don't recognize garbage. They are embarrassed. Water Treatment. That's what they research. I've worked up this fantastic thesis on garbage and they say to me, 'Tasso, none of us are experts in this area.' So!" Tasso lathered the air with his hands again. He poked at the fire with a strangled sheet of newspaper.

"It's the money, Tasso," Nello said. "They don't have a quarrel with you. But all of their research contracts are for Water Treatment." Tasso wouldn't look up from the fire. "If you don't want to play their game you have to find a financial backer, that's all," Nello said.

"I'll get a backer," Tasso mused and winked at Yergos. He grinned. He was still back at the beginning: the Americans drowning theirs, the French vacuuming, the Greeks burying, the Turks piling…

They didn't see Tasso for a while. Nello complained that he took the Engineering Department too personally. Tasso had been down to Los Angeles for a job interview and Yergos wanted to know the results. Nello was too tired to make the visit so Yergos went over by himself. Tasso revved up the fire and brought them beers. He claimed that mountains of garbage were stored just beyond the hilltops that line the Hollywood, Santa Ana and Golden State Freeways, right behind the Hollywood Sign, just out of the motorists' view. The Los Angeles freeways were a movie set, he said, a façade to conceal garbage. It was the Garbage Pile Up Plot. Then he conceded that all the refuse was plowed under at night, when no one was looking, and transformed into those nubbly hills one sees around Los Angeles, growing scrub brush on their crests.

The minute he arrived at the Metta Oil plant Tasso had smelled something peculiar. They had denied it, he said. Later they insisted it was a brush fire in the area. "Brush fire!" Tasso said, "It was the garbage." Tasso got himself another beer, frowning at the fact that Yergos had allowed his own to fizz out. Tasso asked him if he knew of Metta Oil Company. "Metta Oil is required by the government to refine so much crude per year. They would prefer to store it and let the price go up. But they get entitlements for each unit they refine, and they must earn fifty entitlements per year," Tasso explained. "But they can also earn their entitlements for producing methane gas from garbage. Remember my thesis—the dog food? For each unit of methane gas the government gives them one entitlement. They can earn their entitlements through methane gas, keep more oil in crude, and make a profit," Tasso announced.

Yergos nodded and sipped his beer, brooding over this conspiracy. "What did they offer you?" he said.

"They want me to consult part time, commute by plane once a month until I finish my Ph.D. Metta Oil pays, of course. They want me to incorporate their work into my thesis. Once I earn the degree, I go home to Greece for a few months, Metta Oil pays again, then I come back to work."

Christmas passed, New Year's, and Yergos' saint's day. He couldn't wait any longer to find out what had become of the Entitlements Plot. He dropped over after work; Tasso was in his bathrobe. Yergos demanded news. Tasso curled his lip under, shrugged, led Yergos by the elbow to the kitchen chair and began to put business letters down on the table in front of him.

The first letter was from the Chairman of the Environmental Engineering Department at Bolinger University. He said he was sorry but the Department would have to discontinue funding of Tasso's project because all the money had been consumed in the Department's "immediate concerns." Yergos assumed that meant Water Treatment research. The chairman went on to insist that he spoke for the whole Department in urging Tasso to continue his unique thesis project.

The other letter was from Metta Oil. It said that after careful review they had decided not to make Tasso an offer at this time. They said the work in progress Tasso would be engaged in at Metta Oil was of a highly confidential nature and it would not be advantageous to the company if published in a Ph.D. thesis.

Yergos asked Tasso what he was going to do now. "My Belgian tax return came through and I paid off my car," Tasso said. He lit a Kent. "The sanitary landfill people in San Jose want me twenty hours per week." He smoked. "I don't think the Department will award me a Garbage Ph.D.," he said. "I'm the only Garbage doctoral candidate in the whole Department. In the whole world!" He lathered the air with his hands in a gesture of futility. He was sure they were plotting against him.

5. The Weather Buys the Hay and the Weather Sells It

Sotiris rents a forty-five dollar per month apartment, six miles from the center of Athens, and though he lives on the ground floor where the children and garbage trucks wake him up every morning, he does not complain.

His job, making hand-carved wooden furniture, is across the street from his apartment. Next to his job the skeleton of a thirty-foot trimaran squats on supports in an abandoned lot. He is building the boat from his own ingenuity, and plans he bought from a British designer whose name he picked at random out of *Sailboat* classifieds.

Once Sotiris had finished public school and could quit the orphanage, he vowed never to do the things he had been forced to do for so long: go to school, and read. His older brother Yergos, a Physics student at the University of Athens, brought him to the merchant ship he would work on for four months. But Sotiris was just too lonely. Loving the ocean day after day, hoarding his paychecks, pissing into the wind—all this could not sustain him.

Since that stint, Sotiris refuses to go back to the merchant boats. He carves wooden furniture; during the tourist season he helps crew a friend's twenty-foot schooner, shuttling sightseers from island to island. Nothing lonely in that; in fact it has begun to seem like the best thing for him. If he could build a boat large enough to hold eight tourists comfortably on a three-week journey, he would have what everyone wants: a free, simple life, his business, no one to trouble him—just seasick tourists sucking lemons. So he breaks his vow never to read and pores over sailing catalogs; in the process he learns English.

Yergos lives in California now. One day in November Sotiris calls his brother Yergos to say he has taken a cheap Polish flight via Warsaw, East Berlin and Montreal, and will be arriving in California the following morning.

Yergos takes his younger brother to the ports of San Francisco and Sausalito, where Sotiris inspects the sailboats. Sotiris sleeps on the living room floor, his blueprints spread out next to him; he circles the items he needs from the catalog, wondering how he will be able to buy the rigging, afford all of the boat that is beyond the wood he himself can shape, wondering how he can circumvent the hundred percent luxury tax on any equipment or parts for the boat which he buys here in America.

Yergos finds his brother jobs: remodeling kitchens, refinishing wood floors in YMCAs, and building book-cases. At night they draw designs for plumbing systems for the boat, and on weekends Yergos begins to charge the rigging on his Visa card, shipping it ahead to Athens. Sotiris hands over his paychecks to his older brother; he has been here a year and a half now, falling asleep on his blueprints.

For Christmas, Yergos buys his brother a logbook and he buys his brother his ticket home, where apartment, work and dreams are self-contained, where stew can still be bought for ten drachmas, the cook dragging you into the kitchen, you insisting, "This is what I want, this and this," pointing to the pots.

Sotiris boasts of having all he needs now, his job, his half built boat, his apartment, contained in a space of five meters square. He boasts of still knowing tavernas where stew can be bought for ten drachmas.

FORGIVENESS

When Daniel approached me the first time, I had to say no. Sure, Madeleine had been dead for ten years by then, and in the meantime Daniel had been married two more times, and had had four more children. But I hadn't seen him in twenty years, so when he turned up in Santa Cruz, it was as if we were frozen in time, with Madeleine still between us.

I saw his picture in the newspaper, big as life. He looked exactly the same. He had opened a restaurant, called Angela's, and the photo showed him bending proprietarily over a diner's table. I picked up the phone and called Sandy.

"Daniel's in town," I said.

"Oh my god," she said. "For a visit?"

"He opened a restaurant," I said. "On the Pacific Garden Mall."

"Jesus," she said. "Are you going to go over there?"

"I don't know," I said.

I waited a month. Everyone kept asking me, Sandy, my sisters, my boyfriend Wesley, are you going to go over there and see Daniel? Finally I was shopping one day on the Pacific Garden Mall, and I said, *What the hell,* and just walked across the street, through the wrought iron gate, across the cobblestone courtyard, and into Angela's.

A waitress was standing right there, between the cash register and the espresso machine. A refrigerator filled with Pellegrinos glowed behind her. She looked like Madeleine. Eventually it would dawn on me that all the waitresses looked like Madeleine.

"Can I help you?" she said.

"Is Daniel here?" I said.

"Daniel?" she said. "Who's Daniel?"

"The owner," I said.

"You mean Peter," she said.

"Sure, Peter," I said. Peter was Daniel's first name. But Madeleine and I had always called him Daniel. We were the only ones who did. She said it was his middle name.

"Peter's not here," the waitress said. "He's at the beach with Tim."

"Tim's here?" I said. Tim was Daniel and Madeleine's only child.

"You know Tim?" the waitress said.

"I used to," I said.

"They'll be back tonight," the waitress said. "Do you want to leave a note?"

"No notes," I said.

"Can I tell them who stopped by?" the waitress said. She was looking more and more like Madeleine every minute.

"I'll just come back," I said.

Of course I didn't go back. I waited another month. Then, on a very sunny day, a bright, glaring day, a day when I was having a fight with Wesley, and I was shopping on the Pacific Garden Mall, I crossed the street, pushed through the wrought iron gate, walked across the cobblestone courtyard, and let myself in the door of Angela's Café. This time it was Daniel who was standing between the cash register and the espresso machine, backlit by the refrigerator full of Pellegrinos.

He laughed. His eyes twinkled the way they used to when he was up to his usual mischief; when he was about to skewer someone with that sardonic humor of his that was usually delightful, but could oftentimes turn malicious.

"You look exactly the same," he said.

"So do you," I said.

"Do I?" he said. He ran his fingers through his hair and patted down his shirt. He looked at me. I walked up to him and kissed him on the cheek. He kissed me back.

Of course he didn't look the same. He was much more handsome. His hair was shorter, but still dark and curly. He had that freshly scrubbed look. He smelled clean, like soap. He looked voluptuous—the dark curly hair, the

149

white silky skin, the pouty mouth—like that boy in the Caravaggio painting with the fruit on his head.

"Do you live here?" Daniel said. He seemed confused. Distracted. Absent. Daniel had always seemed a little confused, distracted, absent. It drove most people crazy. But I liked it. It gave me room.

"Yes," I said.

"Since when?" he said.

"On and off since college," I said.

"Tim's here, you know," Daniel said.

"I know," I said. "The waitress told me."

Then he put his arms around me and just held me. "I can't believe you look exactly the same," he said.

Of course I didn't. I weighed about twenty more pounds when I was sixteen, my hair was longer, and my clothes were more ragged. Madeleine used to compare me to the fat nurse in *Cries and Whispers* who comforts the dying woman, lying in bed with her, holding the woman's frail body against her ample breast. But I hated to think about that. I didn't realize then that I was fat. I didn't realize then that Madeleine was going to die. And how could she have known? She didn't die for another twelve years.

Daniel used to compare me to Ethel Merman. He said I sang like her, all overly expressive and hokey. Now he sat me down at a table in the back, by the entrance to the kitchen. He made me a cappuccino and brought me slices of freshly baked focaccia bread cut in narrow parallelograms, and stacked like a house of cards on a white saucer.

The entire restaurant was completely white, like a canvas that was primed and ready to be painted on: white walls, white tablecloths, white cotton napkins, white porcelain dishes, white porcelain cow cream pitchers with looped tails for handles, white seat cushions, white candles, white baby's breath in white vases, white salt and pepper shakers. In this sea of white there were buoys of color: the green glass bottles filled with first press olive oil, the blue glass bottles filled with mineral water, gold Raphael angels resting their chins on their hands. It was my kind of place.

While I was sitting there, the third ex-wife, Lisa, swept through the restaurant in a rage, screaming at Daniel, screaming at cooks, screaming at busboys, screaming at all the waitresses who looked like Madeleine. One of these waitresses stopped at my table to whisper to me that the week before, Lisa had stolen all the menus and all the recipes from the restaurant, and had just received a court order demanding she return them.

When she had left and things quieted down again, Daniel came back and brought me a menu.

"So that was the third ex-wife," I said.

Daniel nodded.

"Who was the second?" I said.

"Angela," he said, waving his hand around the restaurant.

"Ah," I said. "How long were you with Angela?"

"Ten years," Daniel said. "On and off. It was rocky from the start."

"And she lives in?"

"Westwood," Daniel said. "With my two daughters. They're in high school."

"And Lisa?" I said.

He looked at the door, where she had just exited.

"Only a couple of years," he said. "That was rocky from the start, too. We have two babies, a boy who's one and a girl who's two. She moved to Marin."

"She's angry," I said.

"She was always angry," Daniel said.

I nodded. I had seen women angry like that many times. Women who couldn't get what they wanted from men. Women who couldn't get men to love them or care for them or treat them the way they wanted them to, women who couldn't get men to sleep with them, or stay with them, or be faithful to them the way they wanted them to. I had been angry like that. Many times. But the first time I was angry like that was not with a man; it was with Madeleine.

I was babysitting Tim, and she came home smelling like Mr. Farnam's cheap drugstore aftershave. I was in the kitchen making tea. She leaned up against me, pushing me into the counter. She reeked of him. "Why did you sleep with Mr. Farnam?" I said. Mr. Farnam was the head counselor where she taught junior high school art classes. She had had a counseling session with him, ostensibly to get over Daniel having left her.

"I didn't sleep with Mr. Farnam," she said.

"Why did you sleep with Mr. Farnam?" I said.

"Why don't I have any privacy from you?" she said.

She walked away then, discarding her clothes on the floor as she went. I followed. They led to the shower. I opened the door, and looked at her, all wet and soapy and naked, her hair plastered down against her face.

"You want to kill me right now, don't you?" she said.

I nodded. I shut the shower door and left.

"Lisa says I turned Madeleine into a lesbian," Daniel was saying. He was still looking at the door.

It sounded to me like a tongue twister: *Betty Batter bought some butter.*

"You didn't turn Madeleine into a lesbian, I did," I said.

"You slept with Madeleine?" Daniel said.

"You didn't know?" I said. I reached across the white table, between the cow cream pitcher and the vase of baby's breath, and put my hand over his.

I had always thought he'd known. His humor was so sardonic, so filled with innuendo, I was always sure he'd known.

"Did you know about Ted? Did you know about Mr. Farnam?"

"You slept with Ted and Mr. Farnam?" Daniel said.

"No," I said. "Madeleine did."

He shook his head. He looked down at the tablecloth. He started laughing.

"I'm sorry," I said. "I thought you knew."

"It's okay," he said. "I left her, you know, for Angela. So it makes me feel less guilty."

Right then one of the waitresses brought us our food—Daniel had Chicken Angela, a grilled chicken breast with green olives, roasted red pepper, fontina cheese, and arugula. It was served with polenta and mixed vegetables. I had the swordfish crepes with shitake mushrooms in a ginger cream sauce. Daniel got up and brought back a bottle of Bargetto Pinot Noir and two wine glasses. He set the glasses down, opened the wine, and poured enough in the bottom of my glass so that I could taste it first. When I did he waited until I told him it was all right, and then he poured us both full glasses. I looked up at him and smiled. He bent down and kissed me on the forehead.

During dinner Daniel asked me about Wesley. He told me Wesley was all wrong for me, that I should drop him and take up with somebody else. Somebody smart as a whip, somebody charming, somebody funny, somebody who would take me to San Francisco and Carmel and Big Sur, and feed me nice meals, and take care of me the way I deserved to be taken care of.

"And who might that be?" I said.

Daniel laughed. His eyes twinkled. He smiled his mischievous smile. He asked me out to dinner.

"We're having dinner," I said.

"On Friday," he said. "At that French place. What's it called? Pearl Alley Bistro? Didn't you live in Paris for a while?"

"When I was in college," I said.

I met him at his apartment. He was renting a studio at the St. George Hotel. His windows looked out over the Pacific Garden Mall.

"Isn't this depressing?" I said.

"Depressing?" he said. He laughed.

"Why don't you move to the beach?" I said.

"The beach?" he said, like he didn't know what that was, or that we were a mile from one. He looked out the window. "But I can walk to work," he said.

He sat on the bed with a shoebox in his lap, and showed me photographs—his children, his wives, when he was a kid growing up in Arizona, when he and Madeleine were together. Then he put the shoebox down on the floor, and lay back on the bed. I sat there and looked down at him. I could have reached out and touched his face or his curly dark hair with my fingertips. I could have bent down and kissed him.

But I didn't. I couldn't get used to the idea that Madeleine was dead, that she'd been dead for ten years. I had begun by thinking of Daniel as my nemesis, as the one who was in the way. I couldn't get used to the idea that that was no longer the case, even though they'd been apart for twenty years. I wasn't sure why. Perhaps because even after he left, something was in the way. Maybe I had always assumed it was Daniel. Maybe I had always assumed that Madeleine had left me because Daniel had left her. Once Sandy said, "Madeleine didn't leave you; you left her. You moved away."

"I moved away, and then she broke up with me," I said. "As she had a million times before."

"You were in a relationship, and instead of staying in town, you moved away," Sandy said. "What did you expect her to do?"

"She could have come with me," I said.

"And you could have stayed," Sandy said. "Admit it." But I couldn't admit it. I hated L.A. I couldn't have stayed there. Not for anybody.

Daniel got up, splashed and dried his face, ran his fingers through his hair, put on his leather jacket, and we went to dinner. We walked over. He tried to put his arm around me, but it felt heavy and uncomfortable, so I unwrapped it, and held it down next to my side with my hands.

We had a Merlot. The waiter poured a little into Daniel's glass, and then held the bottle against his chest while Daniel tasted it. I had a salad of wild greens with pine nuts, gorgonzola and a hot Dijon vinaigrette to start. Daniel had baked asparagus in a puff pastry.

"Why did you move up here?" I asked him.

"My parents live in San Jose," he said. "That's why Madeleine and I bought the cabin in Boulder Creek when you were in high school. Madeleine didn't want to."

"What cabin in Boulder Creek?" I said.

"The one Madeleine and Celeste lived in with Tim and all of Celeste's kids when you were in college," Daniel said. "Didn't you ever go there?"

"No," I said. It hurt me that Madeleine was unwilling to move to Santa Cruz with me when I went to college, but had moved to Boulder Creek with Celeste two years later. I always wondered why they had moved so close to me. Madeleine made it sound like it was Celeste's idea. I had never known that Madeleine owned that cabin in Boulder Creek, or that it had been hers when I was in high school, when I asked her to move with me—hers and Daniel's.

"Why are you shaking your head?" Daniel was saying.

"It's nothing," I said.

"But you're snorting and shaking your head like a little colt," Daniel said.

"Really," I said, "it's nothing."

I was wondering how many of the plays, concerts, and movies they'd taken me to when I was a teenager were really Daniel's idea, not Madeleine's. I was wondering if the yellow Porsche speedster Madeleine and I drove around in all through high school, talked in, made love in, argued in, was really Daniel's, not Madeleine's.

During dinner Daniel asked me how things were going with Wesley.

"Not so good," I said. "He wants me to accept the fact that when he was a child he raped farm animals, but he won't accept that I've slept with women."

"Women have more options," Daniel said.

"How do you figure?" I said. "You have a much wider age range than we do."

"If I had been with a man it would change my life completely," Daniel said. "I couldn't come back."

Madeleine had said the same thing to me when I was in college. She said she didn't see how I could go back to men after being with her. She said she couldn't go back to men after being with me. "But I'm not going back," I said. "I've never been with men."

After dinner I walked with Daniel to his own restaurant. We went inside and sat in the back by the entrance to the kitchen. Daniel made us cappuccinos. The waitresses smiled and stopped by the table, put their hands on my shoulder, bent down and spoke to me in soft tones. I thought about how nice it would be to always be warm, always be fed, always be loved, and always have people around.

"I need a woman who can put up with my eccentricities," Daniel was saying.

"And what are your eccentricities?" I said.

"I don't have much time," Daniel said, "between the three sets of kids, and the restaurant."

"That's not an eccentricity, that's a situation," I said. He nodded.

"Why did you and Angela break up?" I said. "Why did you and Lisa break up?"

"They wanted me to act more emotional," Daniel said.

"I would die right now for a man who wasn't so emotional," I said.

Daniel laughed.

"Really," I said. "I would kill for a guy who wasn't so emotional. I would love that. It would be like walking through a desert, and finding a little pool of water shaded by a palm tree. I'd sit down, lean my back against the palm, touch my fingertips to the water, and splash my face. God, I would love that. I would do anything for that right now."

Daniel just looked at me.

When I was leaving he asked me if I went swimming much. I didn't know what to answer. "Well, maybe you can get back to me on that," he said. "In the meantime, would you like to go swimming with me? Up at school?"

"What school?" I said.

"Your alma mater," he said. "The university."

"Sure," I said. "What time?"

"Six," he said. "I get up at five, and I'm at the pool by six."

"Six!" I said.

"Too early?" he said. His eyes sparkled. He was having a little fun with me.

I kissed him goodbye. "I can't promise," I said.

"No," he said. "Don't promise."

I never met him at the pool. I never met him anywhere, really, except at his restaurant. I brought people in. I still do. I brought my sisters, my sisters with their husbands. I brought Sandy.

I broke up with Wesley, but by that time Daniel had started seeing a florist with three sons. They moved into a house together at the beach. Her name was Lynn or Lorraine or something—some L name. He took her to New York City for Christmas, and to Big Sur for New Year's. I don't know where he took her for Easter or Valentine's Day. They've been together five years now.

Lately I've been going into the restaurant alone to see him, without Sandy, without my sisters. "Tim's not here," he always said. "Tim will be back in an hour. You should call Tim," he said, and wrote down his number for me. Finally I just said to him point blank, "I'm not here to see Tim. If Tim wanted to see me he'd call me."

Daniel asked me over for dinner when I said that, on a Thursday at eight. I showed up. I figured we were going to the Pearl Alley Bistro again, like six years ago, but instead he sat me down at the table at the back of the restaurant, and introduced me to one of the new waitresses.

"This is Gabriella," he said. "I've known Gabriella for thirty years."

"That's impossible," the waitress said. "She's not that old."

"He's known me since I was twelve," I said.

"My god," the waitress said.

"She was one of my first wife's original art students in junior high school," Daniel said. "Her star pupil. Her favorite." He winked at me.

This irked me. I had never thought of myself as Madeleine's student in junior high school. Our affair in high school eclipsed that. Madeleine: I thought of her as the first person I ever loved, the one I always wanted to come back to me, the one who died before she would come back to me.

The new waitress looked down at me, smiled, and put her hand on my shoulder. That's when I realized how beautiful she was: those grey eyes, that blonde hair, that peachy skin, that fresh scrubbed look, that clean soap smell. That's when I realized all the waitresses looked like Madeleine.

The waitress brought us focaccia bread and poured our wine. We looked at the menus as if we had never seen them before. "What looks good to you?" Daniel said. "I'm starving."

"I'm bringing Sandy here tomorrow for lunch," I said.

He put the menu down. "How is Sandy?" Daniel said. "Is she still married? Is she still living up in Boulder Creek?"

"I think you have a little crush on Sandy," I said.

"She's cute," Daniel said. He looked sheepish, like he'd been caught at something.

"Well I'm bringing her in at one," I said. "I made a reservation. I'm telling you so you can get all dressed up if you want, to impress her."

"You didn't tell her I have a crush on her, did you?" Daniel said.

"No," I said. It was a lie. I had told her.

"Because I don't," Daniel said.

"Do you have a crush on me?"

He smirked at me.

"Come on," I said. "I need something. Kevin canceled his dinner and hot tub invitation, help me out here."

"He canceled?" Daniel said. "Dinner and a hot tub?"

I nodded. Kevin was a guy I liked. Another guy I liked. A photographer. I'd known him since college, since I was seventeen. I wanted that, someone I'd known since I was a teenager, someone who felt like home to me, like family; someone from my childhood, from my own back yard.

"Just tell me the truth," I said.

He looked at me, squinted.

"I won't try to sleep with you," I said. "I won't wreck your relationship with Lynn. I promise."

"Lorraine," he said.

"Okay, Lorraine," I said.

"Okay," he said. "So I have a crush on you."

"I'm such an idiot," I said.

"For what?" he said.

"I just wish I hadn't turned you down six years ago," I said.

He looked at me. He took a sip of wine. He looked at the menu. "I think I'll have the Chicken Angela," he said. "That's always a sure thing. Why don't you have the swordfish crepes? You liked them last time."

"Yes," I said. "I always like the swordfish crepes."

"Are you going to have dessert?" he said.

"I don't know," I said. "I'm trying to diet."

"Why don't you have the tiramisu," Daniel said. "Isn't that your favorite?"

I nodded. It was my favorite—the best tiramisu I'd ever tasted.

"What?" Daniel said. "You have a funny look on your face."

"It's nothing," I said. I smiled at him, a fake, forced smile. A deliberately fake, deliberately forced, Cheshire cat, cat-who-swallowed-the-bird smile.

"You promised," he said.

"I'll keep my promise," I said. And I meant it. I would keep my promise.

But I'd always wanted someone who could love me for exactly who I was. Now I believed Daniel was that person, and I'd turned him down. I'd turned him down because he had been Madeleine's husband.

I was such an idiot. I *am such* an idiot.

"What are you thinking?" he said.

"Betty Batter bought some butter," I said. "But she said this butter's bitter. If I put it in my batter it will make my batter bitter. So she bought a bit of better butter, put it in her bitter batter, made her bitter batter better. So 'twas better Betty Batter bought a bit of better butter."

"That's what you're *thinking*?" Daniel said.

"Say it," I said.

"Why?" he said.

"Never mind *why*," I said. "Just *say it*."

HOUSE SITTING

Valerie came upstairs at 9am shouting, "Cindy are you decent? I'm coming up to light the oven!"

Cindy was seated at Louisa's desk with both cats in her lap, trying to write her doctoral dissertation on "Eastern Art and the Concept of Bliss." She had already compiled all the information; all she really needed was to collect her thoughts and write them down. But whenever she tried, she went blank, as if she had no thoughts at all.

"What's wrong with the oven?" Cindy said. She knew it was just a ruse for Valerie to come up and see how she was getting along.

"The pilot light goes out because of all the cockroaches," Valerie said. "Have you seen the roach motel on the counter here? They're all piled up on top of each other trying to get in, like *Yertle the Turtle*." Valerie held a match under the broiler, then got up off the floor and fixed herself a cup of Louisa's decaffeinated coffee. She tapped her cup. "Tastes better than mine." She set the cup down on a cardboard note that said: *USE COASTERS*. In the ashtray she found: *NO SMOKING IN BED PLEASE*. She roamed the living room, hunting for more. "These notes are a new addition," she said, waving one she found wedged into a hairbrush. It said: *SPOTTIE LIKES THIS, GLUM DOESN'T*.

When Cindy twisted away from the desk to look, Glum jumped off her lap, sprung into the sink and sat under the faucet, letting the water drip on his head. "Just look at this place," Cindy said.

"You don't know the half of it," Valerie said. "You should see it after she gets sauced and has a poker party. They say she drinks a whole bottle of Heaven Hill, just to stay awake."

Cindy nodded. Louisa always fell asleep during Thursday night art lectures. Once she had startled herself awake by shouting: *Mr. Walters, I do believe we've been introduced!*, then dozed off again. Since then everyone wanted to know who Mr. Walters was, but they were all afraid to ask.

"I hope you can write your dissertation in this mess," Valerie said. "When I suggested you house-sit I wondered how you'd take to her Bohemian lifestyle."

"I love the Bohemian," Cindy said.

"You do, huh?" Valerie said. "Well how about this: Sometimes when I open the door and look up to see what the Old Lady wants, she's dressed in a shirt. Just a shirt.

166

A seventy-year-old woman. What is she up to?" Valerie went to the landing and looked down the stairs, as if she could find the answer there.

"You're kidding," Cindy said.

"Have I ever kidded you?" Valerie said. "And look." Valerie pointed to the tiny wicker rocker in front of the woodpile. "Too small for a person, too big for a doll. Maybe you can enlighten me?"

"Big enough for a baby," Cindy said.

"You don't put babies in rockers."

"Unless you're Louisa," Cindy countered.

"Probably one of her flea market specials," Valerie said. Once after a successful day at the flea market selling bric-a-brac, Louisa forgot to replace the back window in her station wagon. She drove out of the fairgrounds, leaving a trail of dresses, cake pans and electric can openers on the road. Two men ran after her through the debris, carrying the abandoned window between them, shouting and waving their free hands.

Valerie placed her coffee cup in the sink next to Glum's front paws. He dipped one inside the cup and rested it there, in the tepid pool of coffee. "I'll be downstairs if you need me," she said.

Cindy tapped the pen on her empty notebook and stared out the window at the bay, watching the fishing boats venture out around the breakwater. When Valerie had begged her to house-sit she had said it was the best view in town, and the vast expanse of ocean would soothe her. She would be able to write her doctoral dissertation. No wonder she couldn't work, Valerie had said, in that claustrophobic house she and Michael had lived in before Michael left her and moved across town. Come on, she said, get away from the memories for a while. You'll be right upstairs from me.

Cindy sighed and shut her notebook. She looked at Louisa's bookshelves. The stray papers and upended files bulging with photographs and newspaper clippings intrigued her. Inside a file marked *CHESS*, Cindy found articles about Louisa's son Tommy, a world-ranked chess player. One article said his father was a famous composer. When Tommy was a boy the family threw huge parties on the Upper East Side and summered in a château in the south of France, next door to the Marquis Guy d'Arcangues. Louisa taught Tommy to play chess when he was five and she was graduating from Radcliffe with a degree in Economics.

Cindy poured herself a shot of Heaven Hill, set up the chessboard and played against herself until she became confounded by the arrangement of pieces. She filled the shot glass again and read lengthy inscriptions to Louisa written by famous photographers and economists inside their own books. Cindy had never known anyone famous. She had seen rock stars at concerts, and had once traveled on a plane with a French skiing star. She had also been introduced to a world famous painter at the opening of a friend's show, but that was only disconcerting because she had believed him dead. She just assumed anyone *that* famous must already be dead.

Cindy drank two more shots of bourbon and opened an album of daguerreotypes that said *SNAPS* on the cover. She wished she had had old things at home when she was a child. But her mother died at forty, and afterward her father threw away the memorabilia. They moved to the west coast. After that they never talked about the past, or visited their relatives. The only history Cindy had was the art history she studied, but that was mainly from books and slides.

Cindy looked through the photographs of hilly deserted beaches overgrown with pampas grass, where men in baggy trousers knelt down next to driftwood sculptures and women held up towels between themselves and the camera. She hunted for Mr. Walters. In one photo a man stood beside a dune shack and stared out at the ocean. She wondered if it were he.

"How are we doing up here?" Valerie said when she reached the top of the stairs. "I thought I heard you banging around." She looked concerned. After she made herself a cup of decaffeinated coffee she went to the desk, picked up the news clipping about Tommy and held it close to her face. "Did you know her younger son Alex is illegitimate?" she said.

"So?" Cindy said.

"I don't know," Valerie said. She put her coffee cup down. "I don't think the Old Lady would like it if she knew you had her things displayed like this."

"I know you," Cindy said. "You must come up here when she's not home and rummage around."

"Maybe," Valerie said.

"She's got an Economics degree from Radcliffe. She knows John Kenneth Galbraith. She's got his books here autographed."

"So what? Do you know about this?" Valerie went over to the lamp on the kitchen counter and tapped on the glass. It was filled with water to the neck, and little plastic mermaid baits with hooks floated inside. When she hit the lamp the water sloshed and the mermaids danced.

"What about it?" Cindy said.

"Eugene O'Neill," Valerie said. "They used to go fishing together here in the summers when Louisa was a girl."

"No," Cindy said. "Not with Eugene O'Neill."

"Absolutely," Valerie said. "For squid." Cindy showed her the daguerreotype in the *SNAPS* album. "That might be him," she said.

But Cindy was hoping it was Mr. Walters. "Wow," Cindy said. "Think of all those people she knew. All the events she must have been in on." Cindy had never been involved in anything momentous, or even important for that matter. The boldest thing she had ever done was to take a year off from graduate school in Art History to move to Cape Cod to paint. That's how she had met Michael. But Michael had left her, and all the famous people in town, with whom she had failed to establish ties, had returned to New York for the winter. Now it was October and she had to finish her doctoral dissertation on Eastern Art and the Concept of Bliss. Bliss, she chided herself, what did she know about it.

"She hasn't had a party since she got divorced thirty years ago," Valerie said. "Unless you count poker night for the painters."

"Oh come on," Cindy said. "She's still great. Look at these." She pointed to the newspaper clippings and the photo album.

"Now don't go off half-cocked about Louisa," Valerie said. "I should have known. Remember what you're here for. What are you here for?"

"To finish my doctoral dissertation. To get away from the memories."

"That's right," Valerie said, nodding.

"But look what she managed to do," Cindy said.

"She didn't do anything," Valerie said. "She was just well connected. Now she's not."

Valerie went downstairs. Cindy was hungry; she hadn't eaten breakfast yet. She opened the refrigerator and hung on the door, inspecting all the exotic foods she loved to eat but would never think to buy: capers, goose pate, Mexican chocolate.

That night Cindy left the house wearing Louisa's blue calico dress cinched at the waist with a belt, her black elbow gloves, and velvet cap. Her face was dabbed with Louisa's makeup and she reeked of cologne. She carried a beaded clutch purse containing four ten-dollar bills. She propped a fishing rod with mermaid bait on her shoulder and carried an empty bucket close to her side, so that it knocked against her hip as she walked.

On the way to the wharf she stopped at Costa's Liquors and bought a quart of Heaven Hill. "Nasty stuff, huh?" one of the Costa boys said. Cindy nodded. When Cindy sat down at the end of the wharf and swung her feet over she could see the squid swimming below her. They lit up the water, turning it iridescent silver. She caught them, unhinged them from the mermaids and dropped them into the bucket. She kept the Heaven Hill in the bag and took swigs when the fishing line lagged. She waited for Michael to show up on his evening walk to the wharf.

When he finally arrived he stopped to watch her for a while. Then he peered into the water and remarked in a familiar voice, "There's so many of them it's not even a contest."

Cindy looked up at him. "Hi Michael," she said.

"Cindy?" he said. He still had not recognized her. "I thought you were at Valerie's, writing your dissertation."

"These are Louisa's clothes," she said, plucking at them. "Her son is a world-class chess player. She's close friends with Eugene O'Neill and John Kenneth Galbraith."

"Eugene O'Neill is dead, Cindy," he said.

"But not the caste system," she said.

"You don't have to be upper-class to hang around with interesting people," Michael said. "You've studied artists. What about Auguste Rodin? He hung around with Isadora Duncan and King Edward."

"He was already famous by then. When he was poor he hung around with his pharmacist and baker. He owed them money."

"What about the Impressionists? The Fauves?"

"They got sick, went crazy, and died in the gutter."

Michael looked down into the water and shook his head. "So make something happen." He shrugged, waved, and then stuffed his hands into his jean pockets, shuffling off with his head bowed. He watched his feet move one in front of the other as if he were surprised they propelled him forward.

Cindy walked up the stairs to Louisa's apartment hauling the full bucket of squid. She had positioned two Heaven Hill bottles on top of the load—the empty bottle and a fresh one she'd picked up at Costa's. Spottie and

173

Glum appeared on the landing, poised for attack. They tumbled down the stairs squealing. Glum jumped into the bucket and clawed the squid, while Spottie batted the bucket from the outside.

Cindy cleaned just enough squid for Spottie, Glum and herself. She sautéed them in butter and garlic and set three steaming plates of them—all tentacles and rings—on the poker table with the fresh bottle of Heaven Hill. Spottie and Glum jumped up on the poker table, muzzles perched over the steaming squid, sniffing. While they ate, Cindy dealt a round of cards face up, and played the hands against each other, trying to imagine what Spottie and Glum would play if they weren't such voracious eaters. She tried to imagine the painters sitting around the table with Louisa, and what they would say to her. Cindy had never been invited to the Tuesday night poker games.

Cindy went to the phone and dialed Michael's number. "I did try to make something happen," she said into the phone while it rang. "I moved here. I took up with you. You'd like me if I came from Greenwich instead of Los Angeles. You'd like me if I had a trust fund and felt guilty, instead of having student loan debts, and feeling victimized. We'd still be together, reminiscing about Exeter." But the phone just kept ringing, so she dialed the Rescue Squad. "I think Louisa Ann Emmons just had a stroke or something. But she's wacko so you never know. In either case you better hurry."

"What are you, possessed?" Valerie said when she came up and found Cindy playing poker in Louisa's clothes. She shooed Spottie and Glum off the table, tasted Glum's squid, and bet on a hand of cards.

"Possessed?" Cindy said, "Is that anything like being wacko?" She was listening to the fire horn blow and the sound of sirens coming up the hill.

"Have you started working on your dissertation?" Valerie said.

"Not yet," Cindy said.

"What did I tell you?" Valerie said. "What are you here for?" Cindy looked meekly into her full plate. Valerie looked around at the mess. "I'm sorry," she said. "You really didn't know what you were getting yourself into. Maybe you need a break. Put that squid in the fridge and I'll take you out to dinner."

"I already ate," Cindy lied. The sirens were getting louder.

Valerie looked around the room suspiciously. "You haven't been out all day," she said. "Louisa's got to you."

"I just went out," Cindy said, delighted to say something that was actually true.

"I should have known," Valerie said. "I should have known this would happen. Squid. The wharf. You went chasing after him, didn't you? Cindy, what have I been telling you all this time? Pride. Dignity. Self-respect."

"You don't respect Louisa," Cindy said.

"I can't respect her Economics degree and her friendship with Eugene O'Neill when all I see are the flea market finds and the cockroaches climbing out of the oven."

"But that's now," Cindy said. The sirens were deafening and made her feel as if she were about to be arrested.

Valerie went over to the north window to watch the fire trucks roar by, but the ambulance stopped in front of her house. "My god, here they are," she said. An ambulance driver, paramedic, policeman, fireman and several assistants were beating on the front door. The women went downstairs together and opened it.

"Louisa Ann Emmons just had a stroke," the ambulance driver said with conviction. "We got the call."

"Louisa's in New York City visiting her son Tommy," Valerie said. "Did Mrs. Thorson call? She's a little, well, you know." Valerie tapped her forehead.

"We just take calls from dispatch," the ambulance driver said.

"Well, it was probably Mrs. Thorson across the street," Valerie said. "You should check on her." The ambulance driver didn't answer. "Louisa's in New York. What, do you think we murdered her or something? You can come in and check the house if you want." The men stormed upstairs. "I don't believe this," Valerie said.

Cindy followed her onto the porch. They sat down under the wisteria trellis. When the men charged upstairs,

Spottie screeched and Glum jumped through the north window onto the trellis.

"You've lost it," Valerie said. "I should have known you would do this."

The Rescue Squad came downstairs and shuffled around sheepishly on the porch. "Must have been a crank call," the ambulance driver said.

"You might check on Mrs. Thorson," Valerie said.

"Who's this?" the driver said.

"I'm the house sitter," Cindy offered. The men tipped their hats and started down the walk.

"Let me take you out to dinner," Valerie said. But Cindy wouldn't go. Valerie followed her upstairs, saying, "What are you, out of your mind? Are you really so obsessed with her, or is it just a way to avoid your dissertation?" She tipped the couch-bed onto its back. "Okay," she said. "I didn't want to do this but you're making me. What about this? Look under here."

The couch was falling apart and Spottie and Glum must have found their way inside. They were using the interior for storage. Mixed in among the balls of couch stuffing, chips of broken glass and scraps of food were the pieces of animals and insects: the bodies of bees, moth and bird wings, mice tails, unidentifiable legs and even heads. "Oh my god," Cindy said.

"She's been sleeping on top of that for seven years. This is where she has breakfast in bed, with a little tray over her

legs and the cats sitting beside her begging for food."
Cindy nodded. "Cindy, an interesting life gone sour is not
intriguing. It's trite. Now snap out of it. This is your
moment of truth. So what if the only guy you ever thought
was right for you has just dumped you. The whole world
is waiting with baited breath to hear what you have to say
about Eastern Art and the Concept of Bliss. So buckle
down. Get to work on that dissertation."

"I'm pregnant," Cindy said.

"You're not pregnant!" Valerie said. "Pure diversionary
tactics. Just think: when you finish your dissertation you'll
be out of school for good. You won't have to go back to
the west coast. You can get a curator job somewhere. You'll
meet interesting people. Something important will happen
to you. Something like fishing with Eugene O'Neill or
conferring with John Kenneth Galbraith. I promise." She
went to the bookshelf and took out Somerset Maugham's
Creatures of Circumstance. She reached into the gap where
the book had been and pulled out a small cardboard box.
She shook it close to Cindy's ear. It contained old black
and white photos, two by twos. Valerie set the box on the
coffee table.

"Look through these," Valerie said. "They're Louisa's.
Maybe they'll help you with your work." She took a book
off the shelf and smoothed her hands over the plastic
jacket. "Then read this *Indian Temples and Palaces* all the
way through." She looked at Cindy. "You with me?"

"Yes," Cindy said.

Valerie reached through the gap in the books and pulled out a folder. "And when you're done reading the book you read the letters in this folder," Valerie said. "They're from Alex, her illegitimate son, when he was on a trip to India."

"You do like her then," Cindy said. "She had a life once. It was interesting."

"Okay," Valerie said, "So I like the Old Lady. But she's gone to hell and you will too if you don't finish this goddamn dissertation. And you haven't even had a life yet."

"I know," Cindy said.

"Remember what you're here for. What are you here for?"

"To finish my doctoral dissertation," Cindy said.

"Good," Valerie said. "I'll be downstairs if you need me."

When she was sure Valerie had left, Cindy took a garbage bag from the kitchen and carried it over to the upended couch. She knelt down in Louisa's dress and picked up the decomposing birds and mice with her bare hands. Spottie and Glum rubbed against her side, purring.

Cindy took the Heaven Hill from the poker table, righted the couch and sat down on it. She opened the folder of letters. Inside was a lock of hair, a photo of Alex and an old airline ticket from London to Delhi made out to Alex Walters. "Mr. Walters, I do believe we've been introduced," Cindy said. The old two by two photographs were shots of the Konorak Temple in India. Cindy recognized it at once. The statues portrayed Indians in elaborate sexual positions: oral sex upside down in the hand-stand position, a man having sex with a mule, an elaborate orgy involving eight people. Cindy spread these photographs on the floor and opened the book called *Indian Temples and Palaces*. She knew the book but never bothered to study it because it was discredited as a travel book for tourists, or a coffee table art book, and not considered a work of serious scholarship. She flipped through the pages, and in the chapter on Konorak she found a passage underlined in red ink. It said: *When seen as a whole, the overwhelming effect of the sculpture is not one of sexuality, but one of bliss.*

When the sun was rising and the cats were curled up in the triangles made by her crossed legs, Cindy drank down the last shot of Heaven Hill. She heard Valerie's blender whirring in the kitchen downstairs. Cindy sat swooning on the couch, surrounded by the cats, the empty bourbon bottle, and the photographs of Konorak. For the first time in her life, she thought about bliss.

THE RIGHT THING

for Peter Provencale

Provincetown, 1985

Gabriel Paradise was watching the 1945 French film *Children of Paradise* on his new video machine. It was nearing the end of the movie. After twenty years, the heroine Garance was reunited with her lover, Baptiste. Out on the veranda in the moonlight, she told him that all the time she'd been away she never became spoiled or stupid or ugly because she knew he loved her. *Garance! Garance!* Baptiste said in his sweet, plaintive voice.

When the movie was over Gabriel Paradise turned off his new video machine and twisted his chair around to face the bay. The lobster boats were coming in around Long Point and the terns headed for the sheltered coves in Wellfleet. The silver-blue tint of the water at sunset blended with the after-glow radiating from the large video screen at Gabriel's back. Gabriel Paradise loved his new video machine. "Garance! Garance!" he cried out.

"Sand dune pink, warm coral, pearl gray," a young woman's voice said.

Gabriel turned around. The voice seemed to be coming from the new video machine. "Who's there?" he asked.

"First frost, white sapphire," she said.

Gabriel thought it was the most beautiful voice he had ever heard. He got up and walked over to the video screen. "Who's there?" he asked again. "Who are you?" He looked behind the screen. He walked around it. He opened the closet doors, the bedroom door, the front door, the door to the bathroom, the sun deck. He was looking under the horsehair bed in the guest room when he heard the woman say,

"Emerald, periwinkle, royal silk."

The voice sounded as if it were coming from the video machine. He rushed back into the living room and checked the dials on the machine. The sound was off. The power was off too. "Who's there?" he asked. "Who are you?"

"Amaranth, ivory, midnight blue," she said.

He felt silly, but he thought she might be satisfied and answer his questions if he said, "Taupe, oatmeal, khaki."

"Earth tones are dead," she answered.

"Rose madder, cerulean blue, charcoal gray," he said.

"You used to be a painter," she said.

Gabriel Paradise circled the video screen. "Who are you? Can you appear on the screen?" He unfolded the futon and looked inside for her. He parted the curtains to the fireplace, he overturned the logs; he peeked between the bottles in the liquor cabinets, rinsed out the cognac snifters, anything to drive her out of her hiding place. But nothing worked. "You're beautiful, aren't you?" he said. He was certain of it.

"You better get ready for work," she said. "You'll be late."

"What's your name?" he said. "At least tell me your name."

Gabriel Paradise went out into the garden and cut her a bouquet of wild tiger lilies, Scotch broom, Queen Anne's lace and rose hips. He left them in a bowl on the dining table with a bottle of Cordon Negro champagne that he placed in a silver ice bucket draped with a white towel. He left a pack of Player's Navy Cuts in a clean ashtray with a pack of matches from the Café Magdalena, the little Italian restaurant where he had waitered and cooked for the last fifteen summers. When he was halfway out the door to work he heard her say, "You used to be a lady killer."

Dominic was the manager and head cook of the Café Magdalena and had been Gabriel Paradise's best friend for fifteen years. So when Gabriel tried to conceal his enraptured attitude by addressing it to the fish and pasta, Dominic was immediately suspicious.

"So what is it with you?" Dominic asked Gabriel Paradise as he watched Gabriel wrap the squid lovingly around the exclusive shellfish stuffing and skewer it with a toothpick. Gabriel Paradise placed three stuffed squids into a deep-set crockery dish; then he poured the steaming sauce into the dish. He set the dish with particular gentleness into the oven.

"I'm in love," he said.

"No, you said never again."

Gabriel Paradise nodded his head reverently, and prepared the next order, cannelloni. Now and then he raised his head to acknowledge the waiters who rushed back and forth through the kitchen, grabbing full plates and preparing drinks. When they went out onto the dining floor or deck they slowed down, so as to appear sophisticated, gracious, attentive and, above all, deferential. Everyone thought Gabriel Paradise had been the best waiter at the Café, suave and charming. But a few years before he had retired exclusively to the kitchen; he was sick of the crowds and the bustle he said, he just wanted to cook.

"A local girl?" Dominic asked. Gabriel shook his head in disdain. "From out of town," Dominic noted. "Is she here? Staying with you? At the house?" A mischievous grin spread over Gabriel Paradise's face. Dominic bolted for the phone, but Gabriel caught him and held his hand down on the receiver so he couldn't lift it. "Alright," Dominic said, "is she pretty?"

"Unbelievable."

"Mysterious?"

"Out of this world."

"But you can't be in love," Dominic said.

"Why not?"

"You said never again."

"This is different," Gabriel Paradise said, patting Dominic on the shoulder.

A waiter called across the kitchen for Dominic and he went out onto the floor to answer a customer's questions about the wine list. Gabriel Paradise went back to getting the orders up: fettuccine alfredo, pasta marinara, stuffed flounder, mussels in white wine sauce, pizza rustica, calzones, an antipasto plate; and as he worked he grew more and more content. Everything he prepared looked delicious, life was good, the world seemed to have achieved a new perfection. He caught up with the orders and went out to the edge of the kitchen to get some air, wiped the sweat off his forehead with his apron, and watched the lights from the wharf and buoyed boats flicker against the water.

Long Point flashed its green light, the foghorn was blowing and the telephone was ringing. One of Gabriel's female customers nodded to him from the floor, another raised a finger of approval, another blew him a kiss. He smiled and nodded humbly, leaned against the doorjamb with the insouciant, je-ne-sais-quoi air he knew all the girls fell for. He looked around to see whose table he should pay a call on, whom he should bring home.

Dominic flew past him. "Can't you hear the phone?" Gabriel shrugged, smiled consolingly, and went back to his orders, which had accumulated while he was resting. He wondered how long he'd been standing there, how long the phone had been ringing. Where was the hostess? Shouldn't she answer the phone?

Dominic pushed Gabriel Paradise away from the oven, took the deep-set crockery dish out of his hand, placed it on the shelf inside the oven and shut the door. "It's Angela," he said, "on the phone." He pointed to the hostess station.

"Who?" Gabriel Paradise said.

"It's *her*," Dominic said, "*on the phone*." Gabriel stood there gaping. "Angela, staying at your house, the woman of your dreams, you're in love, remember?"

"Of course," Gabriel said and went reeling to the phone. "Of course." Dominic was watching him, so when Gabriel picked up the receiver he turned his back and faced the refrigerator of wine that stood behind the hostess station. "Angela?" he said, scanning the shelves of wine bottles through the glass doors. "Angela, is that you?" On the other end of the line he could hear Angela breathing, and in the background the theme from Elia Kazan's *East of Eden* coming from the video machine. James Dean's voice was saying something like, *But I just want to see her, she's my mother!*

"Gavi Contratto," Angela said.

It was that voice, that beautiful voice. Gabriel Paradise had never heard anything like it. "Why did you tell Dominic your name when you wouldn't tell *me* your name?" he said.

"Valdadige Pinot Grigio," she said.

"Is your name really Angela?" Gabriel said. "That's a pretty name. I like that name."

"Vino bianco dal profumo finissimo e caratteristico dal gusto fruttato pieno ed armonico," she continued.

"Angela, what are you talking about? Why are you reading me the wine list?"

"Leggermente aromatico," she added.

"Angela, you didn't like the Cordon Negro I sent out for you? Is that what you're trying to tell me?"

"Tenuta Le Velette, Orvieto Classico," she said.

"Is that what you want me to bring home?" he said.

"When are you coming home, Gabriel?"

Gabriel Paradise turned around. Dominic was standing at his left shoulder on the other side of the hostess station. "I get off at 10:30. Do you want to meet me for a drink somewhere?" He winked at Dominic. Dominic pushed his shoulder. Gabriel tried to trip Dominic. Then Gabriel pulled back, frowned, and cupped his hand over the receiver. "Get out of here," he whispered. He took his hand off the phone.

"Don't be silly," the beautiful voice said.

"Oh," he said.

"Secco Bertani, Valpolicella Valpantena," she said.

"I'll be home at 10:30 then," he said.

There was a strange humming on the other end of the receiver. Dominic grabbed the phone away from him. He listened intently. "She must have said goodbye already," he said. "You're gonna see her in two hours." He put the receiver into its cradle and steered Gabriel Paradise back into the kitchen. "It's only two hours," he said, "You'll make it." Gabriel turned to look wonderingly at the telephone. "Why didn't you tell me she spoke Italian?" Dominic said.

Gabriel's mouth hung open. "I—". Gabriel shrugged and went back to the orders. It was all too much for him.

"Lady Killer," Dominic whispered under his breath, and went back to his work.

It was true; Gabriel Paradise was a lady-killer. Everyone knew it. All the men at the Café Magdalena and even those in town agreed that Gabriel Paradise was a lady-killer. If you asked them why they wouldn't be able to tell you. With a good-natured envy they accepted it, acknowledged it, even took it for granted, but they didn't have an explanation. He just was.

The women could tell you why though, easily, and the girls, oh especially the girls, poor things. Gabriel Paradise was charm incarnate: dashing, suave and cynical. He had an innocent sophistication, a touch of Peter Pan that was fatal to young girls. The older women were drawn by his dry wit and nonchalant grace, his deep sensuous voice, the angle of his jaw, which could have been that of an ancient Roman. He created a longing in women that drove them crazy. The men didn't understand, but they believed it, because they saw it happen over and over. Everyone knew that Gabriel Paradise could have any woman he wanted.

So nobody at the Café Magdalena understood when he took up with Debbie. He started to put on weight; he stopped making plans to go to Italy and Spain, to start his own restaurant. They were going to get married.

Of course Debbie ran off with some other guy. Gabriel did not revive his projects or his plans after that. Instead he started to buy comforts for his house: copper bottom pots and the latest electric food processor, special studio lights with remote dimmers, a stereo system with tape player and quadraphonic speakers, and the video machine. He put on more weight. He was still a lady-killer of sorts, dark and quiet, with sad Mediterranean eyes, and he still took home girls whenever he wanted, but never the same girl for very long. And he chose younger and younger girls each time. The last one was only twenty. Now Gabriel

Paradise was thirty-nine, and the woman of his dreams was in his video machine. But she wouldn't come out.

When Gabriel Paradise stepped into his house after work that evening he was overwhelmed by the scent of exotic women's perfume. He had never smelled anything like it before, but it reminded him of wildflowers. In the dining room a Player's Navy Cut cigarette burned in the ashtray. Gabriel inspected the blotches of dark burgundy lipstick on the filter. The Cordon Negro champagne sat uncorked and half-empty on the dining room table. Two burgundy lips were imprinted on the wet rim of the champagne glass—one on the outer rim, one on the inner. Gabriel Paradise poured what was left of the champagne into the glass, fit his lips to the burgundy imprints and drank.

The bathroom was steamy; Gabriel Paradise buried his face in the wet towels and inhaled a lovely foreign smell of almond and rosewater. Talc dusted the dresser-top, and the fogged mirror had been rubbed clear in the middle, leaving zagging sideways streaks.

In the bedroom the bed was turned down, the sheets twisted and the pillows rumpled. The windows stood open, blowing the curtains into the room. The lamp above the bed was turned on, and several moths beat themselves repeatedly against the hot bulb, flying out into the room, turning in an arc and then heading back to the light, building up speed until they crashed into it. The chair had been pulled away from the table, a mirror propped up, and several bottles, glass jars and boxes were assembled there. A woman's silk robe was draped over the rocker and an opened book lay face down in the seat of the chair. Gabriel read the binding that said, *The Memoirs of Jacques Casanova*.

Gabriel Paradise stepped out onto the deck and watched the water flicker under the blinking light at Long Point. He listened to the foghorn blow and tried to anticipate the interval of silence between its soundings. He thought he saw a woman in the garden bend down to pick flowers, then straighten herself, arch her back to listen, tossing her hair in the wind. She was the most beautiful woman he'd ever seen. "Angela!" Gabriel Paradise called out. "Angela!" The woman disappeared.

Gabriel wandered back into the house, sat down on the living room couch and stared into the fire that was blazing in the fireplace. Gabriel Paradise was no Boy Scout and had never been able to build a fire that burned so steadily and spectacularly. His fires always went out. He wondered how Angela did it. She was so handy. "Angela! Angela!" he called again.

"I'm here," the voice said.

It sounded as if it was coming from the video machine. Gabriel Paradise went over to it and stood opposite the screen. Terence Malick's *Days of Heaven* was playing. The heroine had been chasing quail up toward the landowner's house when Sam Shepard, playing the landowner, sat up in the tall grass and said something like: *No, don't run away. What's your name?*

Gabriel turned the sound down and said, "Angela? Is that really your name?"

"Angela, Maria, Carmella, Francesca," she said.

"All those names are yours?"

"Anastasia, Raissa, Hypatia, Octavia," she said.

"Really?"

"Baucis, Chloe, Trude, Clarice," she said.

He felt silly, but he thought he could make her stop if he said, "Ralph, Frank, George, Harry."

"Oh, I see," she said and fell silent.

Gabriel Paradise sat down in the easy chair across from the video machine and tried to puzzle the situation out. *Days of Heaven* was still playing on the screen. Richard Gere was in the barn with the heroine, telling her it was his fault she had fallen in love with Sam Shepard, that Gere had driven her to it. Gabriel realized what the problem was: Angela was like a Genie, but modern. He had to do the right thing, say the right words, press the right buttons to free her. Then she would be his! Gabriel Paradise brooded over the possibilities of what the right thing might be.

The longer Angela remained in the video machine, the more outrageous the rumors about her became. At the

Café Magdalena, Gabriel's friends speculated as to why he would not let his girlfriend out of the house. They had never seen him so preoccupied, so reverent, jumping to the phone before the hostess could answer it. Was Angela so beautiful that his friends would try to steal her away from him?

In town the claims were bolder. Angela was a fugitive from the law; she was a political exile; she was hiding from a previous lover who would be arriving by private yacht to claim her. Many people had gone to the house and caught glimpses of her tending the garden or sitting in the big chair by the window, smoking, drinking champagne and watching old Thirties movies on the video machine like *The Devil is a Woman* starring Marlene Dietrich, or *Rasputin and the Empress* starring all three Barrymores. They had knocked on the front door and heard her call out sweetly that Gabriel was not at home. They were all in love with her.

Gabriel Paradise was humble and congenial, but evasive. He offered profuse apologies for his peculiar behavior, but gave no explanations. When he was not at the Café Magdalena he devoted himself to trying to coax Angela from the video machine.

Despite the fact that Angela stayed in the video machine, Gabriel did not have such a bad life with her. She was attentive and called him regularly at the Café; as far as he knew she hadn't betrayed him with another man

193

while he was at work. When he was home he enjoyed their long talks, Angela in the video machine, Gabriel sitting in the big chair by the bay window, or in front of the raging fire Angela often built for him in the fireplace. Sometimes he would watch old Sixties movies like Godard's *Sympathy for the Devil*, starring Mick Jagger, or *Romulus and the Sabines* with Roger Moore, and Angela would talk with him over the soundtrack. And after the long nights of work at the Café, Gabriel Paradise loved coming home to the smell of the dinner Angela had cooked for herself, the full ashtrays, the empty wine glass, the steamy scented bathroom, the airy bedroom full of moths, the mysterious smell her body had left between the rumpled bed sheets. She seemed to have free rein in the house when he was away, but Gabriel was too discreet to ask her why she retreated to the video machine when he came home. Sometimes he even caught glimpses of her in the garden before she disappeared into the moonlight, and then resurfaced in the video machine. He was almost content with all this, *almost*. He only wanted to look at her face to face, to touch her. Was that too much to ask?

Gabriel Paradise finally gave in. One evening when he was watching Ken Russell's *Women in Love* on the video machine he told Angela that he couldn't go on this way any longer. If she were going to stay in the video machine, he would have to force himself, however reluctantly, to resume a normal life. In other words, he would have to start bringing girls home again. *Women in Love* was ending; Alan Bates said something like, *He should have loved me,* and his wife asked him why he thought he could have both the love of a man and a woman. *Why not?* he said.

"Bastard, rube, curmudgeon, ingrate," Angela said.

"What choice do I have?" Gabriel said. "I've tried everything to get you to come out of there.'

"Not *everything*," Angela said. "Not the *right* thing."

"The right thing! What's the right thing?" he said.

"Part of the right thing is knowing what to do," Angela said, "or figuring it out."

"Oh Jesus Christ," he said.

"Jesus, Mary, Joseph, Mother of God," she answered.

"And that's the other thing—that constant litany of yours. I just can't stand it."

"Oh I see," she said.

"Why do you do it? Why do you always lapse into these recitations?"

"Why, why, why," she said.

"Can't you tell me anything?" he said. "I just want to understand. I just want to do the right thing. I just want you to come out of there. I want to be able to see you, touch you, sleep with you…"

"I want, I want, I want," she said.

"There you go again," he said.

Well, that was that. Angela clearly wasn't going to tell him what to do. So, Gabriel Paradise decided, doing the right thing meant bringing a girl home for the night, and making Angela so jealous she would have to come out of the video machine and stay out, in order to defend her territory against sweet young interlopers. Yes, Gabriel Paradise thought, it was a splendid idea.

At the restaurant that night Gabriel stood in the kitchen doorway wiping his face with his apron and staring absently at the bay. He stopped work often to stand there surveying the boats, and Dominic began to worry. Gabriel Paradise had a melancholy air about him that evening. Had Angela left on her ex-lover's yacht? Why was Gabriel staring out to sea? Dominic searched Gabriel's face; it was full of longing.

Of course the girls loved it. To them, Gabriel Paradise seemed more attractive than ever, with those dark, beseeching Latin eyes, that expression of resigned loneliness. Had Angela really left him? He looked so helpless, so vulnerable. He needed consolation, but from the right woman of course. Donna, one of the right women, smiled understandingly at Gabriel. She was bold and motioned him over to her table. An old friend, she stroked his arm and chatted with him. How were things going? It had been too long since they had last talked. He bent down and kissed her cheek. "I get off work at eleven," he said. "Can we meet for drinks?" Dominic went back into the kitchen muttering quietly to himself, *You devil you, you devil you.*

It was after one in the morning when Gabriel and Donna finally arrived at Gabriel's house. Gabriel found the door unlocked but pretended it was not unusual. As they stepped into the entryway Gabriel noticed a light go out in the living room, and in the darkness he could make out the flickering of the video machine. He went into the living room to see what was playing. The end of Visconti's *Death in Venice* was on the screen. An aging Dirk Bogarde, suffering from a stroke, was watching his unrequited love, the young Björn Andrésen, walk into the glimmering ocean. For a moment Gabriel Paradise was struck with terror—he had not considered the extent of Angela's evil genius.

Gabriel went into the kitchen and poured Donna a drink. She noticed that his recent loss made him sulky and brooding, but that only heightened his appeal. Donna let him keep his distance. She didn't prod him with questions. She believed that men should not be trapped into yielding; they should be enticed.

Gabriel handed Donna her drink and backed her up against the sink full of Angela's dirty dinner dishes. He kissed Donna's neck. "Donna," he said, trying not to sound morose. "Donna."

"DONNA?" a woman's voice thundered from the living room. "DONNA!"

Gabriel rushed into the living room. He unplugged the video machine, the television, the radio, the phone, the stereo system, the special studio lights; he disconnected speakers and headphones, everything he could find to disconnect. Donna had followed him into the living room; and when he turned to her to explain he saw that she was holding a woman's lace camisole in her hand. She had picked it up off the arm of the easy chair. Then he noticed that the entire room was strewn with women's lingerie. Donna went around looking at the slips and bras, the garters, corsets, stockings, lifting them up gingerly, as if with a great love, and setting them down again where she had found them.

"I thought she'd gone," Donna explained gently. "I really wouldn't want to cut in on anyone."

"She *is* gone," Gabriel said. "She's gone. She really has gone." He went to Donna and encircled her in his arms. "Really."

"But—" Donna said hesitantly, looking up into the air. "But that voice…"

"Oh the television, the myna bird—" Gabriel said, and broke away from her. He rushed around collecting the lingerie in his fist.

"The myna bird?" she said.

"The neighbor's pet toucan," he said recklessly, waving his fist full of lingerie around. "*She* did this you know," he said, shaking it at her. "I'm no Looney Tunes. *She* did this." He continued collecting the garments, his back to her.

"I'm sorry," Donna said. "I didn't mean to imply—"

When he had collected all of the lingerie he dumped it in a heap by the front door. "I know," he said. "I know." He led her trembling into the dark bedroom.

Gabriel took Donna's drink out of her hand and put it down on the nightstand. He pulled the bedcovers back and sat her down on the mattress. Then he went around to the other side of the bed, took his clothes off and got in.

The bed smelled of Angela. When he reached over to pull Donna in, he felt Angela wrap her long arms around his waist and slip her sinewy gazelle legs between his.

"Angela!" he said. Instinctively, he reached up and turned on the light. He had been wanting to see what Angela looked like up close.

There was no one in bed with him. Donna sat on the edge, fully clothed, watching the moths fly into the room through the open window and kamikaze themselves against the light bulb. She could hear Bertolucci's *Last Tango in Paris* playing on the video machine. Marlon Brando was saying to Maria Schneider, *In twenty years you'll be playing soccer with your tits.*

"I think I better go," Donna said.

"But she's not here," Gabriel said. "I promise you, she's really not here."

"What difference does that make?" Donna said. She downed her drink and walked out into the hallway. When she was midway through the living room she stopped to look out at the bay. The water looked beautiful in the moonlight. There was a woman standing in the garden, her nightgown blowing around her legs. Donna thought she was exquisite. With a wave of her hand from her lips, the woman blew Donna a kiss. Donna made the same gesture, blowing one back to her.

She was about to leave when she noticed that *The Wizard of Oz* was playing on the video machine. The soldiers were marching up to the castle ramparts. The Tin Man, Judy Garland, Toto, the Cowardly Lion and the Straw Man were surrounded. The witch set fire to the Straw Man and Judy Garland accidentally threw water on her, causing her to melt. The witch wrung her hands and said something like, *How could such an innocent girl destroy my beautiful wickedness?*

Frightened, Donna tried to turn off the machine but when she found that it was already unplugged, she fled the house in terror.

In the morning when Gabriel went into the kitchen to fix his breakfast, he found the dinner dishes washed and a set of dirty breakfast dishes in the sink. The lingerie he had piled by the front door was hanging in his closet. He went from room to room plugging in the lights, clocks, radios, stereo and video machine, reconnecting the wires and speakers.

"That's better," he heard Angela say. Her voice came from the video machine. "Your friend Dominic came to visit this morning," she said. "He had heard rumors in town and was worried about you. I wouldn't let him wake you, but I reassured him."

"I bet you did," he said.

"You better have some breakfast," she said. "You look sallow."

Gabriel Paradise returned to the kitchen and scrambled himself some eggs. When he brought the steaming plate into the dining room he noticed that the end of Nicholas Roeg's *Don't Look Now* was playing on the video machine. Donald Sutherland had pursued the little girl in the red jacket up to the top of the bell tower. She turned to face him, revealing that she was in truth a hideous old woman. She gave Sutherland a disgusted, You-Idiot Look, and slit his throat with a large kitchen knife.

"So I guess that wasn't the right thing, bringing Donna home," Gabriel Paradise said sheepishly.

"I guess not," Angela said over the soundtrack of *Don't Look Now*.

"How's Dominic?" he ventured.

"Fine. He said he'd see you at work tonight."

The movie was over. Not knowing what else to say, Gabriel finished his scrambled eggs under the weight of a complete silence that was so acute it produced a ringing in his ears, and made him feel as if this were his last meal before being sentenced to some painful exile.

Angela was particularly withdrawn and taciturn after the incident with Donna. It took Gabriel several weeks of patient prodding and conversation to get their relationship back to what it had been before he had upset her. He brought great energy and care to restoring their life together, and eventually all was as before: the steamy bathroom, the bedroom full of moths, the sink of dirty dishes, the champagne glasses and full ashtrays, the long talks by the fire, movies on the video machine, the smell of her in the bed sheets, glimpses of her on the deck and in the garden. But once things were back to normal Gabriel immediately grew restless and discontent. Gabriel Paradise wanted Angela to come out of the video machine. For the life of him, he could not figure out the right thing to do.

In town the rumors about Angela escalated to accommodate Donna's evening: Angela had escaped from her ex-lover's yacht and returned to Gabriel. An ex-lover had murdered Angela and her spirit haunted Gabriel's garden. Some people even said they had seen Angela in town, at a local bar, but she remained aloof, wandered off the minute they turned their backs, and disappeared into the crowd. Something was troubling her.

One day when Angela and Gabriel were having a long talk, Angela from the video machine, Gabriel in the easy chair by the bay window, Dominic appeared in the backyard, roamed around the garden as if in search of someone, then climbed the stairs to the sun deck and peered into the living room window.

"Come on in, Dominic!" Angela said casually from the video machine. Gabriel Paradise glared at the screen.

Dominic came through the back entrance into the house. "It's such a beautiful afternoon," he said, "I thought you'd be out in the garden."

Dominic had heard the rumors in town and had come by to find out what was going on. He saw Gabriel every night at work, but his friend had become so reticent Dominic could learn nothing from him. So Dominic decided to come over and see for himself what the situation was.

Dominic used to come over all the time, but when Angela had moved in he stopped, reluctant to invade their privacy. Both times he had come over since Angela arrived he had dropped by without calling first. Gabriel Paradise was certain Dominic was lurking around the garden in hopes of finding Angela alone. It was a trysting place. She was cuckolding him with Dominic. How many times had Dominic come by that Angela had failed to mention? His best friend. Angela was using his own best friend to wreak her revenge on him for bringing Donna home. There is no fury like a woman scorned.

"So where's Angela?" Dominic said. "Didn't I hear her call me inside?" Gabriel shrugged.

"I'm here," Angela said. Dominic looked around. He looked at his best friend, Gabriel Paradise. Gabriel threw up his hands in a gesture of renunciation. "I'm here," Angela said. "In the video machine."

Dominic looked at Gabriel. He went over to the screen. He circled it. He looked at the dials. Dominic's behavior reminded Gabriel of when *he* first found out. His heart softened. Maybe it wasn't an act. Maybe they weren't cuckolding him.

"You *what??*" Dominic said.

"Oh, why did you have to tell him?" Gabriel whined. "I could have said you were in the shower or something."

"We can't keep it from him forever," she said. "He's your best friend."

"I'm so embarrassed," Gabriel said.

Dominic wandered around the living room with his arms folded across his chest, shaking his head. "This takes the biscuit," he muttered to himself, "this takes the proverbial biscuit." All of a sudden he bolted for the doors to the closets, cabinets, and cupboards and flung them open. He ran down the hall, bursting into the bathroom and bedrooms, diving under the beds, parting the clothes hanging in the closets.

"So she's really in there," Dominic said when he came back into the living room. His voice was hedging, as if he were negotiating one of the most important deals of his life. Gabriel shook his head gravely. "So that's the problem," Dominic said.

"I have to do the right thing to get her out," Gabriel said. "But I don't know what the right thing is."

Dominic paced the living room, stopping now and then to stare out the window. Gabriel Paradise was his best friend. He had to help him. "We'll figure something out," he said. "Tell me what else has been going on."

Gabriel Paradise looked around as if seeking aid from a third party, but there was no one else in the room. "When we talk sometimes she goes into these swoons or something where she starts listing things, naming things, I don't know, and I have to break it up. Snap her out of it. It's weird."

"They're not swoons," Angela said.

"What else?" Dominic asked Gabriel.

"Sometimes there's movies playing that I don't have. That I didn't turn on myself."

Dominic turned to the screen. "If I help him, does that still count? Will you come out of there?"

"They're not swoons," Angela repeated.

"A non-answer usually means Yes with women, doesn't it?" Gabriel whispered.

Dominic nodded. "Can she appear on the screen?" he asked.

"Hey," Gabriel Paradise said, "this isn't Disneyland. This isn't *The Wizard of Oz*."

"Okay," Dominic said, holding up his hands as if he were at gunpoint. "So fix me a drink."

When Gabriel came out of the kitchen and handed Dominic his drink Angela said, "Do you know what Anthony Quinn says in *Zorba the Greek*?"

"No," Gabriel said. "What does Anthony Quinn say in *Zorba the Greek*?"

"He says it's a crime against God to refuse a woman."

"Refuse her what? Refuse her anything?" Gabriel said.

"No, not anything," she hedged.

"Well, what?" Gabriel said, quite innocently, his mind preoccupied with how to get her out of the video machine.

"You know," she said.

"You mean—" Gabriel said, astonished. "You mean!" A stifled moan came from the video machine. "Oh honey, Darling, Baby, Mine," Gabriel said. "No one would ever refuse you. Do you think I've refused you?" and he was about to explain that if he could just figure out a way to get her out of there when she said:

"Baby Cakes, Sugar Pie." Gabriel waved his hand impatiently at the screen. He had started her going again. "Butter Ball, Dark Eyes, Little Colt, Wookie, Zi Zi," she said.

Gabriel turned to Dominic and whispered, "You see what I'm talking about? See what she does?"

"Curly Mouth," she said.

"Well answer her," Dominic said. "Go ahead."

"What do you mean?" Gabriel said.

"It's a game. Nicknames. Can't you see? She's playing nicknames this time."

"I can't call her some sickening sweet nicknames," Gabriel said.

"Why not? *You* started it." Dominic clasped his hands together. "Oh Honey, Darling, Baby, Mine," he mimicked in his falsetto.

"That was an excess of emotion, a weak moment. She caught me off guard. I couldn't do it again. I couldn't do it *on purpose*."

"Naming is a form of seduction," Dominic said. "You want her to come out but you won't do what's necessary."

"I can't call her sappy nicknames," Gabriel said. Then he addressed the screen: "Jelly Roll Morton, Dizzy Gillespie, Fats Waller," he ventured.

"I don't see what good that's going to do," Dominic said.

"Duke Ellington, Count Basie, Charlie Bird Parker," Gabriel Paradise said.

"Bop-bop ba-doo-wop ba-bop shoo-waah," Angela said.

They thought they could hear her dancing and snapping her fingers. Gabriel grabbed Dominic's wrist. "This is it, this is it!" he said. "She's coming out!" But the sound of snapping fingers and tapping shoes died away, and the video machine fell silent.

Dominic shook his head. "You refuse to do what's necessary," he said.

It was their night off from the Café Magdalena so Gabriel Paradise and Dominic decided to have a quiet dinner together at the house and discuss the problem. Angela was playing *The Year of Living Dangerously* on the video machine. Billy was telling Mel Gibson that he'd asked Sigourney Weaver to marry him but she'd turned him down.

"Is this prophetic?" Gabriel said.

"I don't think she expects you to ask her to marry you if that's what you mean," Dominic said.

"I Married a Communist, I Married a Monster from Outer Space, I Married an Angel," Angela said.

"Maybe I'm supposed to tell her I love her," Gabriel said.

"I don't think that matters," Dominic said.

"Love and Death, Love Finds Andy Hardy, Love is a Many-Splendored Thing, Love Me Tender, Love with the Proper Stranger," Angela said.

"There she goes again," Gabriel said.

"Gabriel," Dominic said, "it's that game again—movies this time. Aren't you going to play?"

"I'm no hero," Gabriel said. He got up from the dinner table and went behind the screen.

"Maybe she's not real," Dominic said gently. "After all, we've never really seen her."

"I don't believe that," Gabriel shouted from behind the screen.

"Well then," Dominic said, "if you won't do what's necessary to bring her out, maybe you should go in there with her."

"Maybe I should," Gabriel said from somewhere behind the video machine. His voice sounded hollow, dreamy, far away.

"What's your favorite movie?" Dominic said.

"*Children of Paradise*," Gabriel said, invisible behind the screen.

"Angela, what's your favorite movie?" Dominic asked.

Angela didn't answer. She played the end of *Children of Paradise* on the video machine. Baptiste's wife had found him and Garance in their old trysting place. Garance made a move to leave. The wife blocked the door and said something like, *No it's not that easy. You've never lived every day with him, through everything that's petty and boring.*

I have *lived every day with him,* Garance said quietly.

The wife came away from the door and gripped Baptiste's shoulders. *All the time we were together, did you think of her? I have to know, were you thinking of her?* she said.

Garance! Garance! Baptiste cried out. Garance had vanished. He followed her out the door.

"Hey Gabe," Dominic said. "Come out from behind there. She's playing your movie."

Baptiste ran down the stairs and into the street. It was carnival, and the crowd was dressed in costume, dancing. Baptiste spotted Garance and tried to follow her through the crowd.

"Gabe, you're gonna miss the end," Dominic said. He got up and went behind the screen. Gabriel wasn't there.

Baptiste watched Garance climb into a horse-drawn carriage and ride away. The crowd was too thick—he couldn't follow.

Dominic came around to the front of the screen, gripped the sides with both hands and shouted into it, "Gabriel! Gabriel!"

Garance! Garance! Baptiste said as the credits came up.

ACKNOWLEDGMENTS

"Sayings in a Greek Landscape" was published in *Chelsea*. "Forgiveness" was published in *Driftwood Magazine*. "House Sitting" appeared in *Provincetown Women*. Excerpts from "The Gender of Inanimate Objects" appeared in *Shankpainter 22* and the novella was ranked #1 of the top three novellas on the *Zoetrope* website for September 2006. "The Right Thing" appeared in *The Little Magazine*. "In One Enormous Bed Like Children" was published in *Pank*.

I would like to thank Alan Dugan, Mike Curtis, Roger Angell, Greg Pece, Tailwinds Press, Gordon Lish, Don DeLillo, Marcos Karnezos, Lillian Brigman Kane, Adam Davies and Paul Nelson; the Fine Arts Work Center in Provincetown; a Wallace E. Stegner Fellowship in fiction at Stanford University; a National Endowment for the Arts Grant; and writer's residencies at MacDowell Colony, Millay Colony, the Corporation of Yaddo, the Djerassi

Foundation, the Outer Cape Residency Consortium and the Montalvo Center for the Arts.

ABOUT THE AUTHOR

LAURA MARELLO is the author of novels *Tenants of the Hotel Biron* and *Claiming Kin* from Guernica Editions. Her third novel, *Maniac Drifter*, is forthcoming in 2016. *Tenants* was featured in a reading at the Ivana Gavardie Gallery in Paris, France in 2012; *Claiming Kin* was one of five finalists for the Paterson Award in Fiction. Ms. Marello has been awarded a National Endowment for the Arts grant, a Wallace E. Stegner Fellowship at Stanford University, and a Fine Arts Work Center Provincetown Fellowship, as well as Vogelstein and Deming grants. She has benefited from writer's residencies at MacDowell Colony, Yaddo, Millay Colony, Djerassi, The Outer Cape Residency Consortium, and Montalvo Center for the Arts.